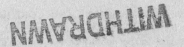

By Meg Cabot

A PRINCESS DIARIES NOVEL

MEG CABOT

The QUARANTINE

PRINCESS diaries

AVONIMPULSE

An Imprint of HarperCollinsPublishers

Brief portions of this book were previously published in another form on the author's website.

Print Edition ISBN: 978-0-06-329193-5
Digital Edition ISBN: 978-0-06-327676-5

Cover illustration and images © Shutterstock images

Avon Impulse and the Avon Impulse logo are registered trademarks of HarperCollins Publishers in the United States of America.

Avon and HarperCollins are registered trademarks of HarperCollins Publishers in the United States of America and other countries.

FIRST EDITION

23 24 25 26 27   BVGM   10 9 8 7 6 5 4 3 2

Author's Note

Warning: This book contains references to the COVID-19 pandemic.

If you'd like to help those in need because of the pandemic, I invite you to join me (and Princess Mia) in supporting the work of VOW for Girls, a growing global movement to end child marriage founded by real-life Princess Mabel van Oranje of the Netherlands. While most weddings are a cause for celebration, the COVID-19 pandemic has put more young girls than ever at risk of becoming brides.

VOW for Girls partners with individuals like us to end underage marriage and support every girl's choice to love on her own terms. One hundred percent of funds raised go directly to local organizations advancing girls' rights. Ten percent of my proceeds of the sale of this book will go to VOW for Girls.

To learn how you can easily donate (or incorporate the cause into your own wedding or other special celebration), please visit vowforgirls.org.

Family Tree of Princess "Mia" Amelia Mignonette Grimaldi Thermopolis Renaldo

Reigning Monarch of Genovia

Dowager Princess Clarisse Grimaldi Renaldo
|
Prince Phillipe Renaldo
married
Princess Helen Thermopolis
|
Princess "Mia" Thermopolis Renaldo
married
Prince Consort Michael Moscovitz
|
Princess Elizabeth and Prince Frank
(Mia and Michael's toddler twins)

Lesser royals:
Princess Olivia Grace Harrison Renaldo
(Mia's paternal half sister)
Prince Rocky Thermopolis Renaldo
(Mia's maternal half brother)
Lilly Moscovitz (Mia's sister-in-law)
Prince René (Mia's second cousin)
Count Ivan Renaldo (Mia's second cousin)

"She had many opportunities of making her mind think of something else, and many opportunities of proving to herself whether or not she was a princess. But one of the strongest tests she was ever put to came on a certain dreadful day which, she often thought afterward, would never quite fade out of her memory even in the years to come."

A Little Princess
Frances Hodgson Burnett

Quarantine Day 1
Royal Bedroom

*J*ust got back from what was supposed to be a routine meeting with the prime minister about my composting program. Considering the fact that compost-treated soil helps protect plants from pests and diseases, and Genovian olive oil is prized throughout the world, it's something we ought to have looked into years ago.

But instead of getting right into my soil treatment proposal, Madame Dupris said, "I've just received terrible news, Your Highness."

Apparently there's a worldwide pandemic.

Excuse me, but *what*??

I mean obviously I did hear a little something about a flu going around in China, but I've been slightly preoccupied with the twins, who are adorable but in their terrible twos (it turns out it's not an exaggeration: the terrible twos really *are* terrible), not to mention ruling a small European principality and of course my composting program and this thing with Harry and Meghan.

But hello? A *pandemic*?

The prime minister says our top public health officer (good to know we have one) is telling her that the only way to contain it is something called "social distancing." This apparently means closing the borders with France, Italy, and Monaco.

Great. Just great. The Genovian Hotel and Restaurant Association is NOT going to be happy with me if I do this, because this is peak tourist season. It's 75 degrees outside, sunny, and absolutely perfect weather for yachting, bocce, dining al fresco, and strolling down the Place du Casino, shopping for luxury goods such as Louis Vuitton handbags and Gucci loafers.

But I knew from my princess lessons from Grandmère not to bother mentioning any of these things to Madame Dupris. A royal is only ever supportive of her prime minister during a crisis. Think of King George and Winston Churchill.

Instead, I said, "Okay, then! Let's do whatever we have to do to beat this thing. Genovia strong!"

"Genovia strong!" the prime minister said.

Then we elbow-bumped one another because Dr. Muhammad, the public health officer, said handshakes are not proper social distancing protocol.

Then I came right home to the palace and poured myself a glass of wine, even though it's only eleven in the morning.

But that's okay. Lots of people drink wine at lunch, especially in Europe. One glass of wine before lunch is nothing. Moderation is the key. Everything is going to be okay. Everything is going to be fine.

Quarantine Day 1 continued
Two Hours Later
Royal Bedroom

Oh. My. God.

Decided to Google the virus. Why did I do that? Michael has told me time and time again to stop Googling diseases.

Why don't I ever listen to him?

I also probably should not have had that second glass of wine before lunch, or that third one while I broke the news to my mother that school will have to be canceled, effective immediately.

We have to cancel school, of course, because Dr. Muhammad says children can be "a serious vector of infection," though of course it's too early to say if this is true of this particular virus. Better to be safe than sorry, etc.

Canceling school does not actually affect me as much as it does Mom, since the twins are still too young for school.

But Mom has Rocky and Olivia to worry about (not that I don't worry about them, too, especially

Rocky, since Olivia is sixteen and a reader and very self-motivated).

Rocky, on the other hand, would happily sit and do nothing all day but play video games, preferably with his friends and my bodyguard Lars, preferably at an excessively loud volume that you can still hear even though the palace walls are three feet thick, made of stone, and they're in another room and wearing headphones.

HOW CAN THIS BE HAPPENING?

And I don't just mean the deadly virus currently threatening my populace. I mean, how can I be a married thirtysomething woman and still living with my parents, half siblings, and grandmother???

And yes, Dad *does* keep promising that Miragnac, the summer palace, is going to be finished "any day now," and that he and Mom and Rocky and Olivia (who is a sweetheart despite now being an age during which I know from rereading my own diaries that I was completely mentally unhinged) and Grandmère are all going to move into it, allowing Michael and me finally to have the main palace to ourselves (as we rightfully ought to have *years* ago, when Dad abdicated).

But I've seen no actual sign of this happening.

Instead, something is always wrong: Dad's contractor can't find the right roof tiles for the parapet, or the turrets are crumbling, or the moat isn't draining properly, or the foundation is sinking, or Grandmère's dog Rommel has developed an allergic reaction to the algae growing in the cistern.

And I know none of this is Dad's fault. It's Grandmère's palace. She's the one who basically let it sit and go to rot since her sisters—my aunts Jean-Marie and Simone—moved out after deciding they preferred living in a hotel in Gstaad, with rooms overlooking the Alps and costing something upward of $2,000 per night. I'd prefer living in a hotel in Gstaad, too, if my other choice was a castle with a sinking foundation and crumbling turrets.

Anyway. I told Mom, "I'm sure this virus thing is all going to be fine! I'm sure it's just a bad flu that will go away in no time!"

"Sure!" she said. "You're probably right!"

And then she grabbed the second bottle of wine we hadn't finished yet and staggered off to her painting studio to enjoy her last few moments of freedom before she has to start parenting Rocky full-time, since she knows as well as I do that Dad will be no help in that regard whatsoever (although he does try, somewhat), and also that everything I was saying about how it was all going to be fine was a lie.

I mean according to Google, it probably *will* be fine . . . after we've achieved herd immunity or gotten a vaccine.

But they had to vaccinate 95 percent of the population in order to wipe out measles, which has an R-naught of eighteen (I know what R-naught means from having watched the amazingly good pandemic movie *Contagion*, starring Matt Damon, Kate Winslet, and Gwyneth Paltrow, so many times. An R-naught is the number of people a single infected person transmits his or her disease to. So that means one person with measles can give it to eighteen other people).

They don't know yet what the R-naught of this virus is, let alone how many people we'd have to vaccinate to keep whatever it is from spreading. But since there's no vaccine anyway, it's kind of a moot point.

The news about the virus was so grim that I decided to Google Genovia instead, because people are always saying such nice things online about their trips to my country. It really does make me feel so good.

This was an even bigger mistake, however!!! Because the first thing that came up was a video of MY GRANDMOTHER and a bunch of her friends and assorted other people I did not recognize dancing on a yacht while wearing very little except extremely large sun hats.

On my yacht. MY YACHT, THAT I OWN. On the dock down the beach from my palace. WHERE I'M WRITING THIS RIGHT NOW.

Then I had to have another glass of wine because these elderly women (who, according to Google, are at an increased risk of death if they contract the virus due to their advanced age) had been spreading their germs all over the EXACT

spot on my yacht where I sometimes let my toddlers play with their toys!

It was at this moment that Michael came home
from the hospital (where he's been supervising
the installation of yet another robotic thingie he's
invented to save people's lives. I'm so lucky to
have such an accomplished and handsome husband who also invents things I don't understand
and puts up with being a prince consort and having to walk three steps behind me at all times
when in public though obviously not when we're
alone).

"Michael!" I cried, running to give him a hug
and have him assure me that everything the
prime minister and Google had said was all a
big mistake.

But instead he threw out his hands to stop me.

"Not only is everything you've heard true,"
he said, looking more serious than I've ever seen
him, "but you can't touch me—I'm a potential
vector of infection now."

!!!!!!!

My husband is a potential vector of infection!!!!
So we can't go near one another!!!!

!!!!!!

Quarantine Day 2
Royal Bedroom

*M*ichael was in direct contact with someone at the hospital who had flu-like symptoms.

So he was told by Dr. Muhammad to come home, strip off his clothes, shower, disinfect his entire body, and quarantine until it was determined if the suspected case at the hospital was COVID-19 or not . . .

. . . which is going to take fourteen days.

I cannot be near my husband for FOURTEEN DAYS!!!!

I'm sorry, but something has to be done about this. Something more than simply closing the schools and borders.

That's why as soon as I drank enough coffee this morning to stop my pounding headache from all the wine I consumed yesterday, I began searching the shelves of the Royal Library for a book that might have a solution. I thought perhaps I might come up with one as brilliant as my composting program.

And after a deep dive into a copy of *The Great Influenza: The Story of the Deadliest Pandemic in History* by John M. Barry, published in 2004 (apparently in 2004, they thought the deadliest epidemic in history was the Spanish flu of 1918. HA! HA! HA! How quaint this sounds now), I thought of something. Something that is probably more helpful than my composting program (although I will return to endorsing composting for every household in Genovia as soon as whatever this is is all over).

Of course my family doesn't agree. They're already annoyed with me for closing the schools and borders (except for Michael, of course, who continues to be a bastion of strength, even as he remains locked inside one of the guest rooms, unable to communicate with me except via phone).

"But I had an oral report due on the life cycle of the iguana," cried my half sister, Olivia, when she learned there'd be no more school.

Honestly, I've never seen a teenager more disappointed that school's been canceled in my life. If this had happened to me when I'd been her age, I'd have been turning cartwheels around the Portrait Gallery (which Rocky was, in fact, doing).

"You can give your oral report to me," I said. "I'll listen to it."

"It's not the same." Olivia isn't the sulky type, but she looked as close to sulking as she could get. "You don't like iguanas."

It's true I did try to have all the iguanas—an invasive species to Genovia, with no known predators—eradicated from the palace grounds, but that isn't because I don't like them. I simply got tired of hearing Grandmère complain about how they were eating all her roses. And the iguanas were, by the way, regularly relieving themselves by the pool in which my toddlers were swimming. According to Google, iguanas can carry disease-causing bacteria.

My father was even more disappointed.

"What about the Genovian Grand Prix?" he asked. "How are drivers supposed to get their cars here if the borders are closed?"

I took a deep breath and broke the bad news: "There isn't going to be a Grand Prix this year, Dad."

He looked as if I'd stabbed him through the heart. But instead of saying anything more, he merely pushed away his (royal chef–made) duck confit uneaten, then got up and walked dejectedly from the table.

Oh, come on. Seriously?

"I suppose the Annual Spring Art Fair is canceled, too?" Mom asked, quietly.

"Not canceled," I said. "*Postponed*. Everything is postponed until we get a vaccine or achieve herd immunity, whichever comes first."

Mom nodded with acceptance. As an artist, she's more used to disappointment, rejection, and loss than Dad—a prince born with a literal silver spoon in his mouth (or at least one that was shoved into his mouth soon after birth)—and can handle it better.

Of course I understand their feelings. It's always disappointing when something you've been looking forward to doesn't happen. How do they think I feel about my composting program? And the fact that it doesn't look as if any of them will be moving out anytime soon?

But this is a global pandemic. How can they be so worried about art fairs and car races?

(Not to minimize their concerns. Art fairs are important, and so are oral reports. I will make sure that Olivia is able to give hers to her class via some sort of video technology. I'm sure Michael knows of something.)

But car races? I've told my dad how much carbon dioxide emissions from motorsports contribute to global warming, and he said, "The day I support Formula 1 going hybrid is the day I go vegan," which means never since he eats animal products for every meal, including snacks, despite the warnings from his doctor about his triglycerides.

Only my good friend Tina Hakim Baba, when I called her, seemed to understand. She is in New York, doing her medical residency. She knows all about this new infection. She even knows about the Spanish flu (which was only called that because the first printed reports of it came from Spain during World War I. The earliest actual recorded cases were at a military fort in Kansas, of all places).

"Do it," Tina said, when I told her about my plan.

"Really? Do you think I should? Because everyone is so—"

"You haven't seen what I've seen. SHUT IT ALL DOWN NOW, MIA."

So I called the prime minister. I told her that now that the news is out that we're closing the schools and borders, and everyone, particularly my family, is already thoroughly annoyed, we might as well close the beaches, hotels, casinos, bars, and restaurants (the smarter politicians, like the mayor of St. Louis, did this during the 1918 epidemic. The dumber ones—like the mayor of Philadelphia, who allowed a huge parade to go on at the height of the pandemic—didn't, and suffered massive mortality rates).

Madame Dupris was quite shocked. "Your Highness, are you sure?"

I said, "Absolutely," and for good measure, I sent her the video of my grandmother, the In-FLUENZer (as I now like to call her), prancing around the marina outside my palace wearing hardly any clothing and without practicing any social distancing whatsoever, as is—it must be admitted—her wont.

"Innocent citizens are going to get sick because of people like her," I said. "It's up to us to stop it."

"But," the prime minister said, "it's high season. If you close the beaches, hotels, casinos, bars, and restaurants, the tourists will leave, and the Genovian economy will suffer."

"Yes. You and I will have to take the responsibility for that. But now is the time to ask yourself, madame, do you want to be the mayor of St. Louis, or the mayor of Philadelphia?"

The prime minister sounded taken aback. "No offense, Your Highness, but neither. I'm quite happy leading the people of Genovia. And while I'm sure both are very nice cities, when I go to the United States, I prefer to visit New York City. I do love the shopping and of course the average New Yorker's outwardly gruff but secretly warmhearted demeanor."

"Okay, scratch that. Would you rather be the mayor from the movie *Jaws* who keeps the beaches open when there's a killer shark out there? Or do you want to be the sheriff who turns out to be right about the killer shark, and saves thousands of people's lives?"

"I have never seen the movie *Jaws*," Madame Dupris said primly. "I prefer romantic comedies."

"Don't we all," I said. "But trust me. You want to be the sheriff. Close the beaches. Close the bars. Shut it all down!"

Fortunately for me the prime minister also has several sweet young children, elderly parents and grandparents (though hers aren't In-FLUENZers), and a smoking hot husband, so she understood perfectly.

"Done," she said, and issued the following proclamation before I could pour my noon glass of wine (honestly I feel like unless you're a health worker or a truck driver transporting important goods like medical supplies or wine or ice cream to afflicted areas, it's okay to day drink alcohol in a time of crisis like this, especially if you have twin toddlers and your husband is self-quarantining in a guest room down the hall and the only way you can see him is to Skype or stand on a tiny balcony and wave).

From Her Royal Highness

Princess Amelia Mignonette Thermopolis Renaldo of Genovia

In view of the very rapid progression of the COVID-19 pandemic, the Genovian government in conjunction with the Royal Palace has decided to close all nonessential public places. The measures announced by the Prime Minister and Princess Amelia may change as the public health situation develops, but until then:

Food shops and markets, pharmacies, tobacconists and newsagents, service stations, medical and veterinarian offices, pet supply

stores, liquor stores, and banks will remain
open. All other commercial outlets and public
places (including hotels, restaurants, casinos,
cafés, concert halls, cinemas, nightclubs,
and beaches) must follow the directives
issued by the palace and remain CLOSED.

If you have symptoms, contact your
physician. Do not go to the Royal Genovian
Hospital or call emergency services. Your
doctor will direct you how to proceed.

Thank you for your cooperation.

—*Her Royal Highness, The Princess of Genovia*

I feel like this strikes just the right tone. I was
the one who insisted on adding the part about
veterinarian offices and pet supply stores remain-
ing open, because think of the pets! My poor Fat
Louie is approximately one million years old and
needs little steps to get up on the bed now when
he sleeps with me and Michael (and Michael is
such a true prince, he says he doesn't mind sharing a bed with the ancient, hair-ball-spewing cat
that I've had since I was a child).

What would I do if the veterinarian was
closed? Or the pet supply shop where I buy Fat
Louie's special food for elderly felines that he so
thoroughly despises?

And obviously we have to keep the liquor

stores open because not everyone lives in a palace like me with a dungeon in the basement that's been converted into a massive, well-stocked wine cellar.

Really, everything is going very nicely, all things considered . . .

Except for the fact that my entire family is now even more furious with me, my husband is in self-isolation, and the major domo just knocked on my door to tell me that my grandmother—the InFLUENZer—wants to see me RIGHT NOW.

Quarantine Day 3
Royal Sitting Room

Grandmère (also known as the InFLUENZer) wanted to know why the Royal Yacht Club is closed.

"Because, Grandmère," I said. "In case you haven't noticed, there is a global pandemic going on. Did you not read the proclamation the prime minister and I sent out, closing all nonessential businesses?"

I handed her a copy but she only crumpled it up and tossed it aside without even reading it.

Typical.

We had the following conversation:

Grandmère: "This is absurd. I go to the Royal Yacht Club every single day for lunch! Rudolfo, the maître d', knows me and always has my Sidecar ready for me the moment I walk in. And the chef has been preparing my lobster Cobb salad exactly the way I like it for years!"

Me: "Well, too bad. The yacht club is

closed, along with every other restaurant
in the country. They'll do takeout, though.
Would you like me to phone in an order for
you?"

Grandmère (tossing her head so
dramatically that her chignon almost
collapses)**:** "Takeout? Royals don't DO
takeout, Amelia."

I could have given her plenty of examples
when our family had, in fact, "done" takeout, including the InFLUENZer herself, but I'd learned
from long experience not to argue with her—at
least over small things.

With my grandmother, it's always best to save
the arguments for bigger things. Like her continuing to want to go out DURING A GLOBAL
PANDEMIC, for instance.

Me: "Fine. Well, we happen to have a royal
chef. Would you like me to ask him to make
you some lobster Cobb salad?"

Grandmère looked as horrified as if I'd suggested she go out in public without her eyebrows
drawn on.

Grandmère: "You can't possibly expect me
to stay cooped up in here, eating *palace
food* every day."

She said "palace food" like someone else might say "prison food." Except that the royal chef trained at Le Cordon Bleu.

Me: "I can and I do. I shut down all the restaurants because of *you*, Grandmère. What were you even doing on the yacht the other day? Someone caught you on video, you know, and posted it all over the Internet."

Grandmère (glaring): "If you must know, I was dancing with Chad and Derek."

Me: "Chad and Derek? Who are Chad and Derek?"

Grandmère: "They're my new friends from Gainesville, Florida. They go to a very fine college there. It's number one in the US."

Me: "You mean the *University of Florida*? You were dancing with spring breakers from the *University of Florida*?"

Grandmère: "Well, I wouldn't know anything about them being spring breakers. They said they belonged to a fraternity, but whether or not they belonged to a band—"

Me: "Grandmère! You know perfectly
well that spring break isn't the name of
a band. It's when all the colleges in the
United States go on vacation for the
second semester! Why were you dancing
with these boys you don't even know? And
by the way, while the University of Florida
is a fine institution, it is *not* number one in
the—"

Grandmère: "Because they asked me to,
Amelia! I could hardly say no. It wouldn't
have been polite."

Me: "Oh, I bet THEY were the ones
who asked you to dance. They were just
strolling along the marina, saw you and
your friends on the royal yacht, asked you
to dance, and the Royal Genovian Guard
just *let* them onto the boat like it was any
other gala to benefit the needy."

Grandmère: "Those poor boys *are* needy,
Amelia. Now that you've closed the
borders, they have no way to get back to
Florida. They were going to take the train
to Paris to catch their flight home. Now
they can't. And because you've closed
all the hotels, they have nowhere to stay
here."

Me (not believing what I'm hearing): "The borders are closed to people who want to *enter* Genovia. Anyone who wants to can *leave*. That was the whole point of the closure."

Grandmère: "But it's very, very cold in Florida right now. Poor Derek has asthma—although you wouldn't know it to look at him, with those biceps."

Me (in shock): "Grandmère. It is not cold in Florida right now. And are you honestly asking if these boys could come live here at the palace?"

Grandmère: "Of course not! I've already invited them. They're getting their things from the hotel. They're going to stay in—"

I'd heard as much as I could stand. Grandmère has done some ridiculous things in her time, but this one took the gateau.

Me: "No. Absolutely not. You're going to call them and tell them they are disinvited."

Grandmère: "What? Amelia! I can't do that. What kind of hostess would they think me?"

Me: "I said no. No more inviting frat boys to the palace or dancing with them on my yacht, okay, Grandmère? You are a member of one of the most at-risk populations, you know. Tina says that you need to—"

Grandmère: "At-risk population? What does that mean? What are you even saying, Amelia? Don't try to talk to me like I'm one of your subjects. I'm a dowager princess and your grandmother. I taught you everything you know about being a royal, and don't you forget it!"

Me: "I'm saying that this is a serious crisis. My husband is in self-isolation because he may have come into contact with someone who has the virus, and he doesn't want to spread it to us or the children. He's making the ultimate sacrifice!"

Grandmère: "Well, that's very noble of him. But I'm making a sacrifice, too, by offering my private quarters to two very young, very vulnerable students from a faraway, very cold land."

Me: "OH MY GOD, GRANDMÈRE! Fine, do you want me to say it? I'll say it: *You're old!*

I don't know how old since you've destroyed
all copies of your birth records, but you brag
about fighting with the Resistance during
World War II as a teenager, so you have to
be in your nineties, at least! In addition to
which you smoke, drink what I can only call
excessive amounts of hard alcohol, hardly
ever wash your hands because you say soap
and water is drying to the skin, and you
never, ever observe social distancing, most
especially with strangers, all of which puts
you in the most at-risk category of anyone
I know. And because I care about you—but
also because I care about my own family,
especially my babies—I am ordering you to
stay here in the palace, without any college
boys to keep you company, and act like what
you are—an elderly woman!"

Grandmère's drawn-on eyebrows had risen to
their limits.

Grandmère: "*Elderly?* You're calling me
ELDERLY, Amelia? How—how *dare* you?"

Me: "How dare I? Because I may be
your granddaughter, but I am also your
sovereign regent and your princess, and you
will do as I say! Now get out of my room! I
have work to do."

Grandmère: "Gladly!"

Grandmère gave another toss of her chignon—
this time succeeding in dislodging it—and did as
I asked, slamming the door behind her.

It wasn't until just now that I realized she took
my last bottle of Italian pinot grigio with her.
Now I'm going to have to ring for more, which
means the staff is going to notice my increased
alcohol intake, which won't be good for morale.
I'm sure Queen Elizabeth isn't over there in her
palace in England, gulping down white wine.

UGH!!!!

NOTE TO SELF: According to John M. Barry, once
the troops at the military camp in Kansas started
shipping out, they began to spread the Great Influenza everywhere. Flu, he writes, has killed
more people in the United States than any other
infectious disease, including AIDS.

God, no wonder Dr. Khan insists I get a flu
shot every year!

I'm thinking of skipping ahead to the end of
this book where they find a vaccine, because this
is super depressing reading.

*M*ichael just informed me (over the phone, since we can't be in the same room) that everyone is *not* cured at the end of *The Great Influenza*.

God! Michael didn't even give me a spoiler alert or anything!

And I still have four hundred and three pages of this book to go (not including footnotes and the index).

Now I know why my dad left this book abandoned in the Royal Library with the spine not even cracked. He appears to have purchased it for some light reading on a trip to Hong Kong (according to a receipt from the airport bookstore that fluttered out from inside the front cover when I opened it). He probably realized it wasn't going to have a happy ending.

I'll keep on reading though because I want to find out how they got the vaccine. Maybe it will help us find one for our virus.

I really hope they didn't have to climb to the

top of a tree in the Amazon like Dustin Hoffman and Rene Russo did in the beginning of the movie *Outbreak* because there's no way I'm getting on a plane right now to the Amazon, not even the royal jet.

Quarantine Day 4
Royal Bedroom

So Michael and I are determined to maintain some sense of normalcy, despite the fact that he's in self-isolation in a palace guest room.

One way we are doing that is by meeting on our respective balconies for a quiet cocktail hour every evening, just the two of us.

Obviously this isn't the ONLY time we're meeting. We meet on our balconies at breakfast time, too, and multiple other times during the day.

But of all the times we meet, cocktail time is my favorite, and NOT because there's alcohol (although that helps), but because the twins aren't there demanding their fair share of "daddy time."

Of course I love Elizabeth and Frank to death, but it's slightly draining trying to pay attention to what Michael is saying while also holding on to the twins' sweet little wriggling bodies in order to make sure they don't fall over the balustrade and into the moat.

But by cocktail time, the twins are usually conked out from their busy schedule of destroying things, so I get pure unadulterated Michael time all to myself. We sit with our feet up, sipping our kir royales, watching the sky turn lavender and pink as the sun sinks into the ocean, listening to the tolling of the church bells down in the village and the lapping of the water below.

Then we say secret things, like how much we love our lives together, and how lucky we were to have found one another, and how nothing, not even this horrible virus or my awful InFLUENZer grandmother, is going to tear us apart.

And then I tell him what a great job he's doing virtually researching treatments and vaccines (he's turning all of the resources of Pavlov Surgical over to COVID-19), and he tells me how proud he is of me for continuing to read the boring influenza book, which he calls "very dry but a highly useful resource," as well as ruling the country (which is nice to hear, since so many people seem to hate me right now for closing down the borders and shutting all the hotels and *especially* all the bars and restaurants and casinos, so that we hardly have any tourists left).

The few that are still here—like Grandmère's new friends, Chad and Derek, whom I've listed as *personae non gratae* at the palace gates, just in case—are angrily scrambling to rearrange their flights or train tickets so that they can leave—especially the ones who were planning to leave by cruise ship, since I stopped allowing those to dock long ago.

Michael says that everything I'm doing makes

perfect sense. It's not my fault that Grandmère—
and so many of the restaurant and bar and casino
and hotel owners—disagree with me.

"It's our busiest time of the year!" my cousin
Count Ivan Renaldo—who happens to own one
of the largest bar complexes in Genovia, Crazy
Ivan's—came over to the palace to yell at me earlier today. "This is when we make most of our
money!"

> **Me:** "I understand that. But in the interest
> of human health and social responsibility,
> we have to shut down so people will go
> home and stay home and stop spreading the
> virus. The main way to beat a pandemic if
> you don't have herd immunity or a vaccine
> is to stay home and avoid crowds."

> **Cousin Ivan:** "But my employees are going
> to suffer! They make most of their income
> from tips!"

I really tried to remain cordial with him and
not point out the number of times he's tried to
commercialize the town with fast-food fran-
chises, steal my throne, etc.

> **Me:** "Well, it was you who chose not to pay
> your employees a living wage or offer them
> benefits or encourage them to save for a

crisis like this one. There are many things
you could do to help them right now, such
as sell off some of your luxury goods and
give them the proceeds. Didn't you just buy
a hundred-foot yacht? I saw it the other
day in the marina—the *Crazy Ivan II*?"

Cousin Ivan (sputtering): "I thought this
country was a constitutional monarchy, not
a dictatorship!"

I let him go on for a while in this vein, since it
was clear he was just feeling insecure about his
own adequacies both as a man and an employer,
until I felt he'd gone on long enough. Then I interrupted.

Me: "You know, Ivan, I was always taught
that it was important to save money for
a rainy day. Well, that day is now. Only it
isn't just raining. It's a full-on monsoon.
Fortunately for your employees, we here
in Genovia are banning all commercial
and residential evictions for the extent
of the crisis, and when they apply for
unemployment, your employees will be
offered all the financial aid they need by
the Genovian government, because we—
and the palace—care, unlike you. Have a
good day."

Ivan stormed away, calling me something under his breath, which my bodyguard Lars told me later was a Russian word for a part of the female anatomy. I won't record it here, however, because I'm a princess. I actually don't mind Cousin Ivan calling me that. I'm proud to be a woman, especially a woman in power, especially one who threatens men like Ivan who measure their own success by the size of their . . . yacht.

It was sweet of Lars to offer to tase Ivan for me, though. I told him not to, however, as that would break the rules of social distancing.

Also, I'm sure Ivan is such a baby, he would call emergency services, which are overburdened enough as it is right now with all of Grandmère's friends calling them, insisting they have the virus when all they have is allergies. The Genovian pear trees are in full bloom right now.

I didn't tell Michael any of this, however. He has enough to worry about, since Dr. Khan, the royal physician, is insisting that he be tested for the virus.

But Michael is insisting (from the balcony) just as strongly that she save the test for the truly needy. As one of the smallest countries in the EU, we also have the fewest tests, something I'm working the phones daily to change.

"I'm not a health-care worker or someone with underlying conditions who might be at risk," Michael keeps saying, looking—I have to admit—extremely fit in jeans and a black T-shirt that fit him in a way that . . . well, let's just say I really do need to go to the palace gym more often to at least *try* to get off some of this baby weight.

But where would I find the time, between the twins and this crisis and making sure Grand-mère washes her hands once in a while?

And Michael says he likes me with a bit of croissant at the waist.

"But you're the prince consort," the doctor keeps pleading with him. "Who knows how many people you've met since you came in contact with the virus?"

But Michael lobbed this zinger back at her over the balcony railing: "None, since I immediately came back to the palace and locked myself in here."

"It's true," I said to the doctor. "He hasn't set foot out of there in four days. And he's having the staff leave his meals at the door on paper plates that he can bag and throw away after use. Not even recycle."

And no composting, even, I refrained from adding, because the whole palace knows I've given composting a rest for the time being (and they all seem strangely relieved by it, even my mother and Olivia, who've been the staunchest supporters. I'm trying not to take this personally).

"Fine," Dr. Khan said, admitting defeat. "But if you feel the slightest hint of symptoms—"

"You'll be the first person I call," Michael said, with a secret wink at me. Because of course we both knew *I'd* be the first person he'd call.

Who would have guessed, when we first met so many years ago at Albert Einstein High School (or was it in his family's apartment, when I was over there to chop the hair off his sister Lilly's Barbies, or something?), that Michael and I would end up here, in Genovia, fighting together against my insane royal family and a global pandemic?

Love is crazy.

Oh, no, here comes the major domo, doubtless with more bad news. I wonder what it could be this time.

Quarantine Day 5
Royal Sitting Room

*L*illy is here!

She is currently spending floor time with the twins (which Dr. Khan says they need a lot of since they currently can only see their father on a screen or from a balcony), teaching them that a cow says moo.

I don't want to be one of *those* parents, but my children already know that a cow says moo. My children know how to open my purse, take out my phone, and order pizza from our local V.I.P. (Very Italian Pizza).

This is what I get for having babies with a fellow New Yorker (who is also a genius).

But even though they're in their terrible twos, Elizabeth and Frank love their auntie Lilly, and are patiently mooing back at her every time she waves the cow puppets she's brought them. Inside, however, I'm sure they're secretly plotting how to steal her phone.

"I still don't understand what you're doing here, Lilly," I said.

"My brother is in quarantine and you, my

sister-in-law, BFF, and the Princess of Genovia, are being sued." Lilly made one of the cow puppets nibble at Elizabeth's nose, which she tolerated, but you could tell it was only because she expected there might be pizza on the horizon. "How was I supposed to stay away?"

"I'm being *sued*?"

"Didn't they tell you? God, I can't believe how they try to protect you from things you really ought to know." Lilly took out her phone—both twins alerted on it like border collies on a flock of sheep—pressed something, and handed it to me. "You're being sued by your cousin Ivan and various other local Genovian business owners for depriving them of their right to earn an income."

"*What?*"

But it was true. An article on RateTheRoyals .com—a website I make it a point never to visit . . . anymore—listed all the ways in which I was despised by many of my own people, merely for being community-minded and trying to protect them from a deadly virus.

I couldn't help saying a word that really oughtn't be said in the hearing of children—at least not in front of a couple of two-year-olds who delight in repeating everything they hear.

"S***!" Elizabeth and Frank cried excitedly. "S***, s***, s***, s***, s***, s***, s***, s***, s***!"

"Oh my God," Lilly said, staring at her niece and nephew in alarm. "When did they start doing *that*?"

"Since they learned how to talk." To the twins, I said, "Hey, you two. Want some pizza?"

Their faces alight with joy, they cried, "Pizza! Pizza, pizza, pizza!"

"My God," Lilly said, even more alarmed. "That's frightening."

"Go ask your grandpère," I said to the twins. "Grandpère would love to buy you some pizza." I knew Dad would love to do no such thing, but he needed all the distractions he could get in order to move past his disappointment about the Grand Prix. Besides, he and Mom are besotted with the twins, and Mom in particular lets them walk all over her.

"Yay, pizzaaaaaaa," cried the twins as they tumbled over one another in their haste to go find my mother and father.

"They're more adorable than ever," Lilly said after they were gone, although she didn't sound like she really believed it.

"No, they're little demons. But they're *my* little demons, and my reason for existing. Except for your brother, of course."

Lilly made the requisite gagging noises all sisters must make upon hearing their brother's praises sung by his spouse, then held her hand out for her phone, which I gave back to her.

"Anyway, I came as soon as I could," Lilly said. "Clearly you're going to need a vigorous defense against these people, and I'm here to provide it."

Lilly has been admitted to the bar in numerous US states and of course here in Genovia as well. It isn't surprising to me that she pursued a career in litigation considering how much she's always enjoyed arguing with people. The only difference is that now she gets paid to do it.

Me: "How did you even get into the country? I thought I'd closed all the borders."

Lilly (smiling a secret smile): "I happen to have an in with the Genovian Royal Guard."

I made my own gagging noises. Lilly and my bodyguard Lars have a friends-with-benefits thing going on that I try very hard to ignore.

"I honestly don't think your services are going to be necessary," I said, quickly changing the subject and pouring us both generous servings of wine. It's much easier to access full bottles now that I've had a minifridge installed next to my bed. What Michael will say about this when he gets out of self-isolation, I can only imagine. "Cousin Ivan will be dropping his lawsuit soon enough."

"Oh, yeah?" Lilly took a big swig. "What makes you think so?"

"Because he was caught with one of his bars open the other night," I explained.

"He *what*?"

"Oh, yes. He had all the window shades down and was only letting people in if they knew the secret password, but he posted the password online, so it wasn't that much of a secret. A devoted patriot dropped a dime on him, and the cops shut the whole thing down in about half an hour." I was actually a little proud of Ivan, since he'd clearly been shamed into the idea by what I'd said to him the other day. "He tried to tell the cops that it was a benefit to raise money for his employees. But even so, we couldn't allow it, since every other bar is obeying the order to cease business. So the police closed him down."

"Wow," Lilly said, gulping more wine. "So what makes you think he'll drop his lawsuit against you?"

"Because if he doesn't, I'll go public with the fact that he endangered public health. And then he'll be kicked out of the Genovian Hotel and Restaurant Association. And he wouldn't want that. It's one of the oldest and most powerful groups in Genovia."

Lilly leaned forward to clink my glass with hers. "Well played, Your Royal Highness."

"Thank you. Like I told the prime minister," I said, "now is the time to be the sheriff from *Jaws*, not the mayor."

"So true," Lilly said, settling back into her chair. "Well, looks like I came all this way for nothing. I wonder what I'll do now." Her gaze strayed toward my bedroom door, outside of which Lars was prowling around somewhere, probably playing video games with Rocky.

I restrained an urge to vomit. "I'm sure you'll think of someone. I mean something."

NOTE TO SELF: After the 1918 parade in Philadelphia that the mayor refused to cancel, it's estimated that half a million people came down with what was then considered the worst influenza in modern history. No one will ever know exactly how many got sick because doctors and nurses were too busy scrambling to stop the outbreak to record the numbers, and the coroner (a close friend of the mayor) was too busy blaming the deaths on the wartime ban on alcohol (claiming that alcohol was, and always has been, the best cure for flu) to count them.

Ingesting alcohol does not, in fact, cure the flu. But in moderation it *can* help you not be as depressed about the way your relatives are reacting to the public health restrictions you've imposed about it.

Genovia has our first official case of the virus!

And it is someone we know.

By "we" I mean Grandmère. Grandmère knows him. Grandmère knows him very, very well.

That's right. The first person in Genovia to come down with the virus (that we know of) is none other than Chad (last name withheld for reasons of privacy), of Gainesville, Florida—Chad, the University of Florida student with whom Grandmère was partying on the royal yacht!

The prime minister says Chad was found by a dog walker (isn't that always how it happens on *Law & Order*?), shivering beneath a towel on one of the lounge chairs at the beach, surrounded by empty cans of White Claw (exact flavor unknown, but I personally prefer grapefruit).

Chad's friend Derek was sitting nearby, eating a calzone and playing *Call of Duty* on his phone. He was not at all alarmed by his friend's condition, but seemed very much alarmed when he saw all the Royal Genovian medical personnel in hazmat suits, who quickly descended upon him and took his temperature.

According to reports, both Chad and Derek surrendered peacefully.

"Fortunately, Chad's symptoms are mild," I told my family tonight at dinner. "And Derek has tested negative. Chad is resting comfortably in an isolation room at the hospital."

"*Chad?*" Grandmère cried, nearly dropping her Sidecar. "*Chad of the University of Florida?*"

"Yes, Grandmère," I said. "Chad. You do know what this means, don't you?"

"Of course," she said. "We must send poor Chad a get-well fruit basket at once. And perhaps some nice magazines. Do we have the latest *Vanity Fair?*"

"No! Well, yes. But just how intimately are you acquainted with Genovia's ONLY coronavirus patient (so far)?"

Grandmère tried to act coy. "Not much. Hardly at all. He and the baroness and I shared a few laughs, and maybe some pommes frites. He didn't seem at all ill, however. He might have said something about his allergies acting up, but you know how the pear trees are in bloom. Everyone's feeling a little under the weather—"

"That's it!" I threw down my napkin. I'd had all I could take. "You're going into self-isolation, too, Grandmère, just like Michael!"

"How *dare* you, Amelia!" Grandmère rose dramatically from the table. "I am no bird; and no net ensnares me: I am a free human being with an independent will!"

I glared at her. "Are you seriously quoting *Jane Eyre* at me right now?"

"And why shouldn't I, when you're treating me as if I were a madwoman? But I won't be locked in any attic. Phillipe, are you listening to a word your daughter is saying?" Grandmère whirled on my dad. "She's trying to cage me!"

"What's this?" Dad finally looked up from his iPhone, where he'd been feverishly looking for sports scores since this whole thing started. But there are none, since all sports have been canceled. "What did you say about a cage, Mother?"

"All I did was make some new friends," Grandmère complained. "I can hardly help that, I'm a dynamic woman, and everyone is attracted to me! And now Amelia is cruelly trying to punish me for it by forcing me to stay in my rooms."

"It's for the public good, Clarisse." My mother tried to help. "You could be carrying the virus and not know it. What if you infected the children?"

"The chances of that are *highly* unlikely." Grandmère reached for her Sidecar. "I had my flu shot this year."

"This isn't the flu, Grandmère," Olivia looked up from her own phone to say. Since we're living through a global pandemic, I relaxed the rule about no phones at the table. In this way, I hope to keep from going insane. "The flu is caused by any of several different types and strains of influenza viruses. This outbreak is caused by one virus, the novel 2019 coronavirus, now called severe acute respiratory syndrome coronavirus 2, or SARS-CoV-2, for which we currently have no cure or vaccine."

Everyone stared at Olivia for several moments.

"Thank you, Olivia," I said, at last. Perhaps I was wrong about allowing phone usage at the table. "That was very informative." To Grandmère I said, "Now do you see why you need to keep to your own wing of the palace, Grandmère? This is a very serious situation."

"But what about Derek?" Grandmère cried. "Who is looking after *him*?"

"Who cares?" I asked. "He's an American college student. He can go back home, to America."

"Uh, actually, he can't," Lilly said, looking up from her own phone. Remember the days when no one had a cell phone, and we all fully focused on one another as we ate? I do. I remember when all I wanted as a teenager was a beeper, for Michael Moscovitz to kiss me, and *not* to be the Princess of Genovia. Well, I got one thing I wanted. "They're not letting people who've been traveling in Europe back into the US. Or rather, they are, but if they've been somewhere that has an outbreak of the virus, they have to self-isolate for two weeks when they get home. Or something. It seems to be changing hourly over there."

"You see?" Grandmère cried triumphantly. "Derek must stay here, and we must offer him our hospitality!"

Now I was certain she was a madwoman. "What? *Why?*"

"Because we're *royals*, Amelia. And that's what royals do. We offer up our homes to strangers in times of duress."

"I am *not* offering up a room in this palace to some college student I've never met who may or may not have the coronavirus."

"But I thought you said he tested negative!"

"He did. For now. But who knows—"

"If Derek comes to stay with us, and I know the sweet little lamb is safe, then I will make the supreme sacrifice, and self-isolate in my own quarters as you suggest, Amelia." Grandmère laid a hand upon her bosom. "Let it not be said that I did nothing for my country during this time of unparalleled disaster and desperation—"

"Oh my God, all right already." I rolled my eyes at the footperson who was standing nearby. "Could you please let the major domo know we need to get a room ready for our new guest, Derek . . . ?" I looked questioningly at my grandmother, assuming she knew Derek's last name.

But of course she did not.

"Derek of Gainesville, Florida!" she cried. "Student at America's number one university!"

Fortunately my own phone rang at that point, saving me from having to continue the conversation. It was the prime minister again. She wants me to give a live televised address to the nation about the virus now that we have our first patient.

Which is all well and good and completely necessary, but. . . .

My hair!

Dr. Muhammad told me under no circumstances was I to let anyone who hadn't been screened for the virus come near me, and that includes my hairstylist, Paolo.

Obviously hair is the *last thing* anyone should be thinking about at a time like this.

But one does want to look good for one's country, even during a crisis.

Quarantine Day 7
Royal Bedroom

I did my own hair and makeup for my televised address to the nation, giving them the news that we have our first official case of the virus.

Michael watched it and said (via FaceTime from self-isolation) that I looked great. Which is lovely, but he *has* to say that, since we're married.

Paolo was not so complimentary. I just got the following voice mail from him:

"Principessa, why you go on the television and you do not call me, Paolo? You hair, it look no good! So many roots, and the split ends! You make Paolo look bad. Next time you call me, I do not care about the germs. Ciao."

Paolo isn't the only one who's mad. I also announced a shelter-at-home order because too many Genovians have been going out. Obviously not to bars or restaurants, since those are all closed, but to have picnics at the beach—even though the beaches are closed—and especially onto their yachts to have extremely large parties—including hopping from boat to boat—without practicing any social distancing at all!

Do people think that because they're out on the water, the virus goes away? IT DOES NOT.

I understand that people still want to have fun, in spite of the virus, but can't they do it AT HOME and IN SMALL GROUPS?

What choice did they leave us but to issue the stay-at-home order?

Honestly, I don't know what they were expecting. They can complain all they want about this being a "nanny" state, but I am only thinking of their own health and safety.

Besides which, Genovia could never be a "nanny" state. It is obviously a "princess" state.

I think I did a pretty good job of illustrating this during my address, especially during the hand-washing directive. All Genovians must wash their hands AS MUCH AS POSSIBLE (and take their RINGS OFF, or they will develop a rash. Not that this has happened to me. Okay, it has) for twenty seconds, or the time it takes to sing to themselves the entirety of the Genovian national anthem.

Because so many Genovians do not seem to know the national anthem, I had my film crew air it during my address, so everyone could be sure to get the words right.

But unfortunately because we were working with a skeleton crew due to the virus, and also keeping a six-foot distance from one another, and no one thought to check one another's work, what aired during my national address was footage from one of the unauthorized biopics of my life.

So everyone got to see a video of the glamorous actress who plays me in the unauthorized movies of my life, right alongside me, in my pandemic hair.

Oh, well, whatever. It's pretty clear that during a time of crisis like this, things aren't always going to go right. Everyone should be allowed at least one do-over. As long as no one dies or otherwise gets hurt, who even cares?

And I've decided that I like my pandemic hair. It's a look I might keep forever, along with my pandemic yoga pants, extra snuggly overlarge sweater, and Birkenstocks, which I now wear all day long (except when doing formal addresses to the nation and virtual meetings, during which I swap out the sweater for a more princessy look on top).

Why did we as a society even bother to dress up before? I do understand it for balls and more formal occasions, but if you think about it, it makes no sense the rest of the time to worry so much about how we look. What is even the point?

Although I can't say I'm entirely thrilled by the beard I can see that Michael is growing. I'll have to wait until I can touch it before I make my final decision.

Oh! The day I finally get to touch Michael again! Only . . . how many more days? *Seven?* Can that even be *right*?

Time is going by so slowly. Or is it quickly? Dr. Muhammad warned me during our weekly COVID-19 update that people's perception of time can change during a pandemic for many reasons. One, because we're all so stressed, but two, because our normal schedules have been disrupted, and we have less social interaction. So time can seem to pass more slowly, or more quickly, depending on the individual.

"But it's still important," Dr. Muhammad said, "to make plans for the future. Because there definitely *is* a future!"

I was a little surprised at how emphatically she said that last thing—as if someone had questioned whether there might be a future. *I* certainly hadn't. In *The Great Influenza*, the author describes how they literally had *no clue* what they were doing medically—you didn't need a college degree or even to have seen a single patient to become a doctor in 1918—and most people survived. We have so much of a better chance at beating this. Of *course* there's a future!

Our future might just look a little different than the one we used to live in. In the future, people who used to always greet one another by kissing on both cheeks (sometimes twice) will probably not do this so much.

And, with luck, people who used to shake hands as a form of greeting might stop doing this, as well, in order to avoid spreading the virus.

That would be fine with me! I'm tired of having

my hand crushed by certain male world leaders every time we meet to discuss important issues, such as global climate change (and then having those same world leaders dismiss my very legitimate concerns and talk about golf instead).

I won't miss that *at all*.

*M*y ex-nemesis Lana Weinberger just called.

I refer to her as my "ex-nemesis" because we buried the hatchet my senior year in high school when Lana apologized for her atrocious behavior toward me, and even explained the childhood trauma she'd suffered that had engendered the behavior (not that that excused the behavior. Many people suffer much worse traumas in childhood and don't go around bullying others the way Lana did).

But I forgave her, because that's what princesses (and self-actualized people) do, and we've been friends ever since.

It helps that she's made a concerted effort not to be as shallow as she used to be, especially now that she's married to a decent guy (who just happens to be a Rockefeller and a multimillionaire) with whom she has an adorable daughter—Purple Iris, so named in honor of Blue Ivy, the firstborn of Lana's idol, Beyoncé. Lana recently gave birth to a son, whom she of course named "Sir."

Even though Lana is *trying* not to be so shallow, that doesn't mean she always succeeds. That's why she was calling, as a matter of fact:

Lana: "Mia, would you care to explain to me why the pilots of my private jet just told me that they can't file a flight plan to Genovia? I thought we were all getting together for Easter, like we do every year. But they're saying your country is *closed*, or something?"

Me: "Oh, yes, sorry, Lana. I meant to call you sooner. I have to cancel our Easter plans. We're having a viral pandemic here. From what I understand, there's one going on in the US, too."

Lana: "Oh, *that*! Yes, I heard about that. But it only makes old people sick. We're young. *We* don't need to worry about that."

Me: "Uh, no, Lana. It isn't just old people who get it. It can strike anyone."

Lana: "No, only if you live in like, Los Angeles or Brooklyn, or something. But not where we are."

Me: "Lana, we have a case here in Genovia."

Lana: "Oh, *one* case. Mia, you were always
such a hypochondriac! You closed your
whole entire country for ONE case?"

Me: "Yes, Lana, because I don't want
other people to get it. We're trying to
flatten the curve before things get worse."

Lana: "But it's not like we're even going to
do anything while we're there except what
we always do, which is go to the beach and
drink wine while our nannies watch the
kids."

Me: "Lana, I've closed all the beaches,
and my nanny, Alba, left. She has elderly
parents who need her, so I sent her home
to be with them."

(While still getting full pay, I'd like to add. But
I'm a princess, so of course I can afford it.)

Me: "But my mom and my little sister are
generously helping out with the babies right
now, thank goodness."

Lana: "What? Oh my God, Mia, how
terrible for you. Fortunately I still have my
au pair. She's amazing—a student at NYU
studying dance, only of course now all of
her classes are by something called Zoom.

Don't even ask me how anyone can learn dance online—so she can travel anywhere with us, as long as there's Wi-Fi. She'll be happy to watch all the babies for us while we sit on your yacht and drink pinot grigio."

Me: "I'm so sorry, Lana. The yacht is in dry dock getting completely disinfected because the person who has the virus was seen dancing on it with my grandmother and her friends."

Lana: "Ew, really? Well, we can hang at the pool, then. I don't care, Mia! Just *somewhere* that's warm where someone else can watch the kids while we celebrate Easter the proper way, with pinot and Peeps."

Me: "Lana, I can't. You know I can't. I have to be a good example for my country. I told my citizens that they have to observe social distancing and shelter at home, so I have to do the same thing. Did you know Michael has been in self-isolation in one of the guest rooms for *eight days now*? *I haven't seen my husband in eight days.* Well, I mean, I've *seen* him, but I haven't been able to *touch* him, or be touched by him."

Lana: "God, no wonder you sound so tense. Anyway, Mia, that is just ridiculous. You're taking this whole thing too far. We can most certainly still come for Easter if we all place our lounge chairs six feet apart. And the dining chairs in the Royal Banquet Hall as well. God knows it's big enough."

Mia: "No, Lana. Dr. Muhammad, our public health officer and the lead member of my Genovian Coronavirus Task Force, says it isn't safe for people to be traveling at the moment, even on a private plane. And besides, it isn't just the beaches that are closed here. All the bars and restaurants, clothing stores, jewelry and shoe stores—*everything* is shut down. I don't think you'd enjoy a visit here. So you're better off staying home and protecting yourself and your children and your au pair."

Lana (practically crying): "But I've been cooped up inside with these kids for the *whole winter*! Except for when we went to Disney, back when it was open. I just can't stand it anymore! Did you know it was *forty degrees* here the other day? Whoever even heard of such a thing? It's supposed to be spring!"

Me: "I'm sorry about the weather, Lana. I'm sure it's awful there right now in your huge mansion in the Hamptons right on the beach."

Lana: "The *cold* beach."

Me: "Right, the *cold* beach. But you still can't come here. It's for your own good."

Lana (sniffling): "All right. I guess. But can we get together some other time, when this is all over, and have wine by the palace pool?"

Me: "Of course, Lana. I promise. When we get through this thing—and I swear to you, we're *going* to get through this thing, because Michael has gathered a team of very smart scientists together and is throwing all the resources of Pavlov Surgical into finding cures and vaccines for this virus—we will get together for wine by the palace pool."

Lana (sounding more cheerful): "Okay! Well, I have to go re-do my makeup. It's all smeary now from crying. Love you. Bye!"

Me: "Love you. Bye."

Although of course I was lying to her. Not about loving her—I do, even though she can be so irritating sometimes. I was lying about the other part:

I'm starting to not be totally sure we're going to get through this thing.

We were all eating lunch (Grandmère seated a socially distant six feet away because she's still refusing to self-isolate even though she was caught on film partying with Chad, Genovia's only positive patient—so far) when we heard a blood-curdling scream from the Grand Staircase.

It sounded inhuman, and we soon saw—when we all ran in there to see where the sound was coming from—that it *was* inhuman. Fat Louie, my very old cat, was sitting at the top of the staircase, yowling.

"Louie!" I breathed a sigh of relief that it was only him and not some ghost who lives in the palace that none of us had ever noticed before (not that I believe in ghosts. Much). "What's wrong with you?"

"That cat is getting dotty in his old age," Grandmère said, which is rich, coming from her.

"He doesn't look right," my mother said.

That's when Fat Louie let out another scream,

then opened his mouth and let loose a stream of vomit the likes of which I have never seen (and I have twin toddlers).

All cats vomit. It's what they do, the way dogs—like Grandmère's dog, Rommel, who is now completely hairless and also mostly blind—lift their legs and pee on every tree and fire hydrant they pass.

Only cats mostly simply vomit up hairballs and the occasional meal they've scarfed down too quickly.

That is not what Fat Louie did upon this occasion. On this occasion, Fat Louie vomited up a river of what appeared to be pool water and undigested cat food, all of which came streaming down the steps of the Grand Staircase towards us, gaining more and more momentum the closer it came, like something out of *The Shining*.

"Look out!" Rocky cried, diving for cover behind a suit of armor. "It's a gusher!"

"Dear Lord, the babies!" My mother rushed to protect my twins, who were gazing upon the wave of liquid cascading toward them in wonder.

"Oh my God!" shouted my father. "That carpet is five hundred years old!"

"This is fantastic." Lilly had her cell phone out and was filming, most likely to post on her Tik-Tok, which has millions of followers. "Can you get him to do it again?"

"The poor cat." Only Olivia had the appropriate reaction. "What did he *eat*?"

It was difficult to get up the staircase to check on Louie because the steps were so slippery, and there were so many flecks of chicken giblets coating them.

But when I did finally reach the beleaguered feline, he was thoughtfully licking a paw, looking as if he didn't have a care in the world.

"Oh my God, Louie," I said. "What did you do?"

"He's got it!" Rocky cried, from behind the suit of armor. "He's got the Rona!"

"Don't be silly," I said. "Cats can't get it."

"They can," Olivia assured us, reading from her phone. "But the odds are very low. Judging by the fact that most of this food appears to be undigested, I suspect something else, such as an intestinal blockage."

My mother gasped. "Could he have eaten a sock?"

We all turned to stare at the cat, who had now started licking his other paw, looking extremely pleased with himself. Fat Louie had, in his youth, been famous for eating entire socks, resulting in expensive surgeries at the vet's office to remove them.

But he seemed to have learned a lesson and given up the practice later in life. We'd all also become much better about leaving our socks lying around. Some members of my family—

like Grandmère, for instance—no longer even wore socks, because they considered their feet so attractive, and wore only open-toe shoes that allowed their diamond-encrusted pedicures to show whenever they could get away with it.

"No," I said. "No, he wouldn't have done that."

What I meant was, "He wouldn't have done that NOW, during a global crisis. What kind of cat would be so thoughtless as to eat a sock NOW, when the world is in such total disarray and we all have so many other things to worry about, and I personally have an entire *country* to worry about, not to mention a family that is bonkers and a husband I haven't been able to touch in days, after not having eaten socks for years?"

Then it hit me. Of course. Of COURSE Fat Louie had chosen this exact moment to go back to eating socks.

Because cats don't care what is going on in your world, the world, any world. To cats, everything is about them. Not caring about anything but themselves is what cats *do*. It's why we love them (well, that and the cute way they snuggle up to us, when they choose to).

"Order the limo," I said, scooping up my very satisfied-looking cat. "And call the vet's office! I'm taking Louie in."

My mother gasped. "But, Mia, you can't! You yourself issued a shelter-in-place order!"

"For all nonessential travel. This is essential!"

"I'll say so." My dad was still gazing glumly down at the floor. "This carpet is ruined."

"Oh, Dad, who cares about the carpet?" I was making my way back down the stairs while cradling a purring Fat Louie like a baby. It was very hard to see over his enormous belly and not slip on the bits of food and pool water that he'd so skillfully expelled from it. "A life is at stake!"

"I'm aware of that," Dad said. "But I'm not even sure this carpet is insured. It's from the sixteenth century. It's a historic piece, and most likely priceless."

"Dad, cool it about the carpet! Did anyone call the vet?"

"Yes." As usual, Olivia was the voice of reason. "They're open and between surgeries, and can squeeze him in. But apparently they do not consider a cat vomiting one time an emergency."

I was appalled. "Did you tell them it was *projectile* vomiting? Down a staircase?"

My dad was even more appalled. "In the *royal palace*? And that most of it landed on a priceless heirloom of historic importance?"

Olivia regarded us both calmly. "I said he has a history of sock eating and might have an intestinal blockage. I didn't say the part about the historic heirloom. They said due to COVID-19, you're to wait in the car. They'll come out and take Louie in his carrier into their office and run tests on him."

I breathed a sigh of relief. "That's fine."

Fat Louie remained relaxed and purring in my arms, not seeming at all sick . . . right up until the moment I attempted to place him in his pet carrier. Then he suddenly realized what was happening, stiffened, and began to yowl, resisting with all of his might.

"No," I said, and grunted as I peeled each one of his claws from my chest. "You . . . must . . . go . . . to . . . the . . . animal . . . hospital."

Finally he gave up and relented to being stuffed into his carrier, perhaps realizing that there were consequences to his actions—or perhaps not, since he was a cat.

"Who is going to clean this mess up?" my father demanded as I was going out the door, with Serena, Olivia's bodyguard—Lars, my own bodyguard, was still out looking for Derek, Chad's friend and possible co-infector, who had managed to slip past authorities once testing negative. It's extremely unlikely that during a pandemic anyone will try to assassinate me, but you never know. My cat had already most likely eaten a sock, and no one was expecting that, either.

"I don't know, Dad," I said. Most of the palace staff had left to be home with their own families, which was perfectly understandable. We are down to only a few footmen and footwomen, the major domo, the chef (thank God), and a skeleton crew of the Royal Genovian Guard. "I have slightly more important things to worry about at the moment. Why don't you clean it up yourself, since you're the one who's so worried about it?"

Dad did not like this answer at all. "*Me?* Clean it myself? It's not MY cat!"

"Well, it's not your palace anymore either, is it?" I snapped at him. "So it shouldn't bother you, then."

"Ho ho!" Lilly cried, and even my grandmother looked impressed. She raised her Sidecar and said, "Cheers to that."

But I don't know what she's toasting, since she was supposed to move out ages ago as well.

During the drive to the vet's office, I felt a bit guilty over being so short with Dad—in between dreading what I was going to find out when I got to the animal hospital. Louie really is too old to risk going under anesthesia. So I texted with Michael to tell him what happened (I'd have FaceTimed, but I didn't want Serena and the chauffeur to overhear).

Fortunately, Michael was on my side (as a decent spouse should be). He texted back:

> **Michael:** It's time your parents moved out, anyway. I love them, but they really need a palace of their own.

> **Me:** I know. Of course this pandemic is only going to further delay the construction on the summer palace.

Michael: Of course. Did Louie really vomit pool water down the stairs?

Me: I'm pretty sure it was regurgitated pool water. You know how much he's been drinking from the pool lately. It could have been moat water, of course, but it seemed cleaner.

Michael: Which carpet did it land on again?

Me: The one with the snakes and virginal maidens.

Michael: Oh, good. I always hated that carpet.

Me: Me, too. Louie actually has very good aim for a cat, it turns out.

Michael: As much as I've always hated that carpet, I've always loved that cat.

Me: And I've always loved you. I can't wait until you're out of quarantine.

Michael: You can't even imagine the things I'm going to do to you when I get out of quarantine—

Unfortunately at that moment the limo pulled up to the animal hospital. I called to let them know we'd arrived, and they told me that the vet would be out to discuss Louie's case with me—or that if I wished, I could come in, but they preferred that only a single person entered at a time, to minimize everyone's risk of infection.

I turned to Serena. "I'm sorry," I said. "You have to stay in the car."

She looked extremely alarmed. "But, Your Highness—"

"It can't be helped. Fat Louie is my firstborn and as much a part of my family as any of its human members. I can't let him face this alone. But I can't let you risk becoming infected. I'm going in without you."

Then, before she could stop me, I leaped from the limo and, Fat Louie yowling in his carrier beside me, raced into the animal hospital.

They could not have treated me—or Louie—with more kindness. And I don't think it's because I'm the princess of the land in which they live and work, either. I think that people who go into the medical profession—whether to treat people or animals—are just kind, caring people. That is certainly true of my friend Tina Hakim Baba, who is working on the front lines of the battle against this infection in New York City.

The veterinarian at the animal hospital in

Genovia checked Fat Louie out all over. Fat Louie behaved disgracefully the entire time, hissing, growling, and generally acting the opposite of the way he does at home. There was no sign of the sweet, loving cat who lets me hold him like a baby, rub his belly, and kiss his face.

When the doctor was finished with his exam, he said, "Well, I don't see any signs of a blockage, but he has lost some weight, which in any other cat would be worrying, but in a cat Louie's size—"

I wanted to say, "How dare you?" like Grandmère, but I knew what he meant, so instead I said, "Maybe you should take full-body X-rays, as well as a full blood panel." I got all of these fancy medical terms from a lifetime of watching television shows such as Grey's Anatomy, ER, and Chicago Med, and also from looking up diseases I could possibly have on WebMD.

"Um, yes," the veterinarian said. "I was going to say I won't be able to tell for sure without an X-ray. I don't think full-body X-rays will be necessary—I'm not even sure what that is. But we can also take some blood and run some tests. If you'd like to wait in the comfort of your vehicle, Your Highness, while I take Louie back and do those things—"

I decided it wouldn't be strictly necessary or wise for me to escort Fat Louie into the X-ray lab, so I agreed to wait in the limo for him.

Serena was still fuming when I got there.

"Princess," she said. "You put me in a very difficult position just now by going off your own! What if there was someone in there who wished ill of you?"

"Ill of me? You mean who wanted to assassinate me?"

"Yes!"

"Well, there wasn't," I said. "They were all very, very kind. Don't you find that people in the medical field are always very kind? It's just like on *Grey's Anatomy*—"

"I'm not speaking of people in the medical field! I'm speaking of someone outside the medical field who could have learned that you were going to be there, and plotted to come at the same time and cause you harm."

I used some hand sanitizer that we had in the limo, not even for this particular pandemic, but for use after I'd been shaking hands with the populace in general.

"Serena," I said. "It's okay to worry. But maybe don't worry so much. It's going to be all right."

"How?" she demanded fiercely. "*How* is it going to be all right?"

"Because of what I just told you. We have amazing, incredibly kind, and smart medical personnel who are working round the clock to keep us safe. We have scientists who are doing the same thing, only they're working to find vaccines and maybe a cure. All we have to do is give them the support they need, and do our best to stay home and not get sick ourselves if we can possibly help it. I believe I spoke about this in my national address." I tried not to sound impatient that I had to remind her of this. "It's okay if you missed it."

"I did not miss it. It's just that, begging your pardon, Your Highness, but you did not stay home and do your best not to get sick just now."

"Well, this was essential business."

"Because your cat vomited?"

"Yes! Life still has to go on, Serena. People are going to have to walk their dogs, or take their cats to the vet, or go to the store to buy toilet paper, or wine if they don't have a wine cellar in their dungeon. They're just going to have to do it carefully, like we did just now." I glanced out the window. "Oh, look, here he comes!"

The vet was coming out with Fat Louie in his carrying bag. Serena wouldn't let me pop out to get him. She did the popping, placing a much more subdued Fat Louie inside the limo on my lap.

"Well, the X-ray was clear," the veterinarian said to me through his mask. "No blockages of any kind, such as the, er, socks you were telling me about."

I sagged with relief. "Oh, thank goodness. But then why he did throw up like that?"

"His thyroid levels are off since the last time

we measured them. That would explain the weight loss. You said he was drinking a lot of water?"

"Obsessively, from the pool."

"Cats experiencing hyperthyroidism can behave in manic ways."

Hmmm. I wonder if hyperthyroidism could explain my grandmother's behavior, too? My whole family's, actually.

The vet gave me some medicine for Fat Louie's hyperthyroidism and some special food for his sensitive stomach, and also explained that he'd given the cat some anti-nausea meds and subcutaneous fluids, just to make sure he was okay.

"Fat Louie," he said kindly, "should be feeling better soon. Call me if he's not."

"Thank you so much. I hope we're *all* feeling better soon, Doctor," I replied.

You could tell Fat Louie was sorry for the trouble he'd caused by the way he stuck his head out of his carrier and looked curiously at the deserted streets of Genovia as we drove home. Everyone was observing my shelter-at-home order—everyone except for me—which was heartening to see.

When we got back to the palace, the first thing I noticed was that all of Fat Louie's vomit had been cleaned up.

"Who did that?" I asked, as Fat Louie jumped from his carrier and headed immediately out to the pool—not to drink from it, but to sit by it in the sun and lick himself all over, disgusted by the indignity we had put him through.

"Dad," Olivia informed me. "He cleaned up the whole thing himself. Well, Grandmère helped a little by telling him what to do and pointing out all the spots he'd missed."

"Aw," I said, touched. "What a lovely mother-son activity."

My dad, as far as I knew, has never cleaned up anything before in his life. This was definitely a first.

"He thinks the carpet can be saved," Lilly told me, "since most of what came out of Fat Louie was water. Your dad's going to put it in his own palace, if it ever gets finished."

"Good," I said. "And good riddance!" I wasn't sure if I meant the carpet or my dad. On the whole I think I meant the carpet. Of course I did!

Then I went upstairs to wash my hands for twenty seconds while singing the Genovian national anthem, and to tell Michael the good news about the cat via the balcony (since I couldn't tell him up close).

Only five more days . . . !

Quarantine Day 10
Royal Bedroom

Despite some news reports to the contrary, Genovia is still holding steady at only one (1) COVID-19 patient (a spring breaker from Gainesville, Florida).

Chad (last name withheld for reasons of privacy) is in stable condition at the Royal Genovian Hospital, resting comfortably and in good spirits. The hospital has been inundated with gift baskets of pears and olive oil for him from well-meaning Genovians.

People seemed determined, however, to push up our numbers. We've had to close the airports and marinas and establish checkpoints on all roads leading into Genovia, and ask car owners to present proof of residency before they can enter—that's how many people are trying to get in!

I've always known, of course, that Genovia is popular. It's certainly where I would want to be during any sort of international crisis. The beaches are lovely (though they're all closed now) and the weather can't be beat, and of course we serve every flavor of gelato that you can imagine (when the shops are open).

But you would think people would take into account that our hospital is quite small. We barely have enough beds for our permanent residents, let alone visitors! And our ICU is tiny. If the worst were to happen, we only have enough ventilators for twenty patients.

In *The Great Influenza*, John M. Barry writes that in 1918, communities such as St. Louis that chose to "lockdown" experienced far fewer deaths than those that did not (like Philadelphia), simply because their medical facilities were not stretched beyond their capacity.

How can no one not understand the logic behind this?

Chad has only been allowed to stay because he was here before the lockdown occurred, and because he's ill. Chad's roommate, Derek, meanwhile, had to be tracked down by the Royal Genovian Guard. He was finally caught outside Crazy Ivan's (currently acting only as a liquor store and not a bar, and so has permission to be open as an essential business) and is now being well taken care of by . . .

Me.

That's right. We have a University of Florida student living with us here at the palace, because my grandmother says the only way she'll stay in self-isolation is if we "look after poor Derek."

Obviously, I've stuck him in the little guest

apartment above the pool house (like Ryan Atwood on *The O.C.*, but let me tell you, Derek does
not look like Ryan—or perhaps I've been married too long to a full-grown man to appreciate
the looks of nineteen-year-old boys, with their
smooth hairless bodies, ubiquitous tattoos, and
weak chins), because it's the room farthest away
from our quarters. Not to be mean, but I do not
even know this boy.

And although he's tested negative for COVID,
who knows what other diseases he could have?
I saw the way Grandmère was grinding on him
in that video someone posted of the two of them
"dancing" together.

But even though I've put Derek as far away as
humanly possible from the rest of us, I still have
to *hear* him all the time, because he's already
managed to figure out how to work the outdoor
sound system over there.

"What *is* that?" I asked Michael this evening
while we were enjoying our nightly cocktail on
our respective balconies (only FOUR more days
until he's out of self-isolation!).

"I believe that's 'Baby, I Love You' by Aretha
Franklin," Michael replied.

"But *why*?" I was shocked. "*Why* is he playing
that *now*, outside? And so *loudly*?"

"I'm guessing because he's a college student,"
Michael said, not looking nearly as aggravated as
I felt. "And because he likes it. And because he's
getting to live for free in a beautiful apartment

above a swimming pool in a palace in Genovia, with all the free food and booze he wants. So he's showing his appreciation."

"Well, *I* don't appreciate it. I'm putting a stop to it right now!" I jumped to my feet.

"Why?" Michael asked.

"Because the whole town is going to hear that!"

"So what? The whole town is in lockdown, unable to go out. They might enjoy hearing the Queen of Soul coming from the palace."

"But—but—he might wake the babies!"

"Who cares?" Michael was laughing. "There's a beautiful sunset, nice music, and we're together—at least as together as we can be right now. Why don't you just relax?"

I stared at him in disbelief.

Here is the problem: I love my husband, but I *hate* being told to relax. I can and will relax, but only when I'm good and ready. Don't *tell* me to relax.

And especially don't tell me to relax when there's a deadly pandemic and thousands of people are trying to enter my country, but I can't let them in (which I feel very guilty and conflicted over), I have twin toddlers, a psychotic grandmother, a cat with hyperthyroidism, a principality to rule, and some random college student living in my pool house, playing VERY loud music during the only time I'm able to enjoy the company of my self-isolating husband.

I was about to tell Michael how very much I hate being told to relax (which he *knows*) when something strange happened:

Derek—who obviously fancies himself some kind of DJ—put on his next song for our alleged enjoyment: Stevie Wonder's "For Once in My Life."

And I felt myself . . . relaxing.

I was ACTUALLY relaxing. During a global pandemic.

I don't know how. Or why.

It was all so strange, because I'd just been talking to Tina on the phone—poor Tina in New York City, where they're having one of the worst outbreaks of the virus, and Tina is bravely working night and day to combat it—and she had JUST been saying to me that in addition to our physical health, we need to look out for our mental health during this stressful time as well, in whatever way we can, whether by:

- Finding some kind of hobby or project we enjoy (Ha! Yeah. Right!)

- Exercising (seriously?)

- Meditating (please)

- Watching a movie or television show (who has time for this? Though Tina does, apparently—she is re-watching *Friday*

Night Lights on Netflix for the thirtieth time in between shifts, and I am thankful to Netflix for broadcasting *Friday Night Lights* to help those like Tina who are out there on the battle lines)

• Reading (honestly, this one I get. Especially for people like Tina, lover of all things romance. I just wish John M. Barry had elaborated more on the *interesting* parts of the Spanish flu in his book—like that during the height of the pandemic, when hospitals became so overcrowded they could no longer admit patients, some American families resorted to *kidnapping nurses* and forcing them to care for their loved ones. Mr. Barry gives this incredibly fascinating fact only *one sentence* in his book, when I could read an entire *series* about only this! Why hasn't some author written this series already? Why didn't Catherine Marshall, author of one of the greatest books of all time, *Christy*—later made into an Emmy Award–winning TV movie starring Tyne Daly and Kellie Martin—write about some nurse getting kidnapped by a handsome wealthy farmer to care for his sick child, and eventually falling in love with him? Even though of course if this happened in real life, it would be a sex crime, and end up on an episode of *Law & Order: SVU*)

- Whatever else helps that is not illegal or harmful to ourselves or others

I assured Tina that I'm journaling every day (well, almost), but as a busy working mother—even with a lot of help (despite Alba, the nanny, departing)—I barely have time to care for my physical health, let alone my mental health.

But I'm not even the person doing the worst in my family right now, mental health–wise. You would think that prize would go to my father or possibly my grandmother (although her mental health is so bad that she thinks she is the sanest person in the family and often brags about being so). No. Oh, no.

Today I found out that that prize goes to my half brother, Rocky. Because today I found out that Rocky got into a fight.

With a swan.

One of the swans from the moat.

A LIVE SWAN. *My little brother got into a fight with a SWAN.*

I can't imagine what people who live in a regular-sized house or apartment are going through if they, like me, are sheltering in place with young children. It's difficult enough in a palace.

In any case, the swan appears to have won, since Rocky has a black eye, and I saw the swan a little while ago, strutting around and waving his wings like Creed after a prize fight.

Mom was busy helping out with the twins and Dad of course was yelling into his phone about his investments, so I was the one who was forced to sit down and have the following talk with my little brother:

"Rocky," I said. "Can you please not beat up the swans from the moat? They're only birds. You're a human boy, and much smarter than they are."

Rocky: "But he started it!"

Me: "Yes, well, he may have started it, but it's up to you to put an end to it."

Rocky: "I tried to! But then he hissed at me, and hit me in the eye with his beak!"

Me: "I know. But he's only a swan. He didn't know any better. HE IS A BIRD."

Rocky (sullen): "None of this would be happening if it weren't for this stupid virus. I was supposed to be playing in the Genovian Youth Soccer National Championship this week, and instead I'm cooped up in this stupid palace with these stupid swans!"

Suddenly, everything became much clearer. I have no idea why the Royal Genovian Academy is taking so long setting up online classes. But there hasn't been a peep out of them yet except to say, "We will be contacting you soon!" and meanwhile, the kids are running around wild, beating up swans because their minds aren't being actively engaged and their mental health is literally going to the birds.

Although I have a feeling things are going to get worse when they DO set up the online classes.

Me: "All right, listen, Rocky, I understand. There are a lot of things I'd rather be doing this week, too. But the Genovian Youth Soccer National Championship is going to get rescheduled. I promise. In the meantime, if you could just try to get along with the swans, I'll give you—well, I'll give you anything you want."

Rocky (considering this): "Really? Anything I want?"

Me (realizing I was making a huge mistake but thinking, *How bad could it be?*): "Sure."

Rocky: "Great. I'd like my own sword, please."

Me (I should have seen this coming): "No. You cannot have a sword."

Rocky: "Then can I have my own flame thrower?"

Me: "No. No, you cannot have your own flame thrower. Ask for something reasonable that is not a weapon with which you can hurt swans or people."

Rocky: "Fine. Then can I just play soccer with that guy Derek who moved in above the pool house? He said he'd play with me if you said it was okay. Please?"

Me: ". . ."

Rocky: "PLEASE???? You said anything. I saw him dancing with Grandmère in a video, so it's not like we're not friends with him. He's cool, he likes soccer and video games. He says he's studying music history at the best college in the USA, University of Florida, so that he can be a DJ one day."

Me: "Fine. Yes, you can play soccer with him if you don't touch the ball. Or him. Stay six feet away from him at all times."

Rocky: "THANKS! I will!"

I wish I could go back to the days when playing soccer with someone was all it took to make me happy. Actually, those days never existed for me.

Suddenly the music shifted, and Derek began to play "Take Me to the River" by the Talking Heads.

"See?" Michael said, tapping his fingers along the stone balustrade. "Isn't this nice? Aren't you glad you gave it a chance?"

"Okay." I had to admit Derek had all right taste in music. Not GOOD. But all right. "But if this goes on past Rocky's bedtime, I'm shutting it down."

Sometimes being the Princess of Genovia isn't so bad after all.

*L*illy just told me I'm working too hard (although I wasn't working, I was reading. But reading about millions of people who died over a hundred years ago in a deadly pandemic counts as work because if we don't learn from the mistakes of the past, how will we make the right choices in the present?).

"Come have some popcorn with me," she said, "and watch *Tiger King*."

Me: "Lilly, I know you're trying to take care of me, but I don't have time to watch a documentary. I have too much work to do. And if I did have time to watch a documentary about people who make extremely poor choices in life and then end up in jail, it would obviously be any of the many documentaries about the Fyre Festival."

Lilly: "Well, I personally can't stomach watching a bunch of privileged people complain about their accommodations at a sybaritic music festival not being luxurious enough. Let's watch the classic deadly virus disaster film *Outbreak* instead."

Me: "Again, I have no time to watch movies, and if I did, it certainly wouldn't be *Outbreak*."

Lilly: "Oh, really? Why not? A little too close to reality right now?"

Me: "No, that movie is nothing like reality! I know now from reading *The Great Influenza* and also from our lived experience that if a deadly virus broke out, it would take at least months and possibly years to get a cure, if ever, not days. It's because if I wanted to watch a movie about an apocalyptic event, *Night of the Comet* starring Catherine Mary Stewart and Kelli Maroney as teen survivors of a comet that has turned almost everyone else on earth into either zombies or dust is a far superior disaster movie. It has makeovers."

Then Lilly started arguing that I had no taste in apocalyptic films, so we made the following list (during which Tina Hakim Baba FaceTimed and added her own opinions):

Lilly, Mia, and Tina Hakim Baba's List of Favorite Movies/Shows to Watch When You Want to Get Your Mind Off a Deadly Pandemic That Is Actually Occurring (or Really Any Time):

Lilly: Obviously *War of the Worlds*— both the Tom Cruise version, because he runs a lot and it's always fun to see Tom Cruise running, and the newer version on the Epix channel starring Elizabeth McGovern, because it's hilarious to see Lady Cora from *Downton Abbey* shooting guns during an alien invasion.

Mia: Wrong. Obviously the best disaster movie to watch right now is *The Crazies* starring Timothy Olyphant because a) zombies in a small town, and b) Timothy Olyphant is the sheriff of that small town. Although the ending is not my favorite.

Tina: The ending is horrible! Wouldn't you rather watch something gentle and soothing, like *Enchanted*, in which a princess falls from her fairy-tale world into ours and possibly falls in love with a commoner instead of her handsome prince, and there are cute kids and animals and a totally happy ending?

Lilly: Ugh, no. Let's watch *Armageddon*, in which a giant meteor is hurtling toward the earth and NASA has to hire a ragtag band of oil drillers to land on the asteroid and split it apart and save the planet.

Mia: First of all, I love *Armageddon*, but nothing that happens in that movie is realistic. I mean, I get it, that's part of what's fun about it—I, too, enjoy Owen Wilson, not to mention Bruce Willis, in just about everything. But if you want to watch a *realistic* disaster movie about an asteroid hitting the earth, obviously you should watch *Greenland* starring Gerard Butler, or even *Deep Impact*, which premiered the same summer as *Armageddon*, both of which are more accurate portrayals about what our governments would do in such a catastrophe, which is completely screw everything up. Plus *Deep Impact* stars Téa Leoni, the amazing actress from one of the best shows of all time, *Madam Secretary*, which is about a woman bravely leading her country in a time of crisis, and which is also what we should all be watching right now instead of having this conversation.

Tina: Speaking of shows we should all be watching now, do you watch *The Good*

Place? That's a really great show about
a woman who thinks she's in heaven but
actually—well, I won't spoil it for you, but
you should really watch it, the love story
is so—

Lilly: Um, no, Tina, because I'd prefer
to see *Contagion,* in which Gwyneth
Paltrow is one of the first victims of a
deadly virus and Kate Winslet a fearless
epidemiologist determined to save lives!
Plus Matt Damon has to battle food
shortages and a teenaged daughter
who doesn't want to social distance.
It's basically the life we're living now,
only if we weren't in a palace and the
government was actually organized and
semicompetent. Obviously I don't mean
YOUR government, Mia.

Mia: Thank you. But that is why I'd prefer
to watch *Anna and the Apocalypse*—a
much funnier version of almost the
exact same story but with zombies AND
it's a musical AND it takes place at
Christmastime—

Tina: Oh, that sounds fun! But if we're
talking musicals, I think I'd rather see *Sing
Street,* that movie about the teenaged boy
in Ireland who starts a band to impress a

girl? It's so sweet and funny . . . and since
I've been watching the hilarious *Derry
Girls* on Netflix, it sort of fits that same
vibe.

Lilly: No, thanks. What about *Carriers*?
How can you resist a hyperrealistic zombie
road movie starring Piper Perabo from
Coyote Ugly and Chris Pine who played
your boyfriend in the second unauthorized
biopic of your life, Mia?

Mia: Um, very easily, because instead I
would watch *Ozark* starring Laura Linney
and Jason Bateman, both of whom are
great in everything. Jason Bateman was
fantastic as a possible child killer in *The
Outsider*, too. And I love Laura Linney
every time she introduces anything on
Masterpiece Classic.

Tina: You know what else would be
great for us to watch together? *Zootopia*,
the uplifting animated story of a young
country bunny struggling to make it as a
cop in the big city. You guys, I cried so
many times while I was watching it . . .
with joy.

Lilly: You know what would make me cry
with joy? If we watched *The Andromeda*

Strain, in which a deadly extraterrestrial microorganism falls to earth and begins killing everyone who comes into contact with it and a team of scientists have to figure out how to destroy it before it kills everyone on the planet. There's a book, an extremely bad TV miniseries, and a movie version.

Mia: Would you please stop? How about instead we watch *Independence Day*, in which the same thing happens but it's actual aliens who begin attacking the planet, and Will Smith, Bill Pullman, Jeff Goldblum, and Vivica A. Fox have to team up to save the planet? Or *Attack the Block*, where aliens invade a South London apartment complex, but only a young John Boyega (of *Star Wars* fame) and Jodie Whittaker (from *Doctor Who*) know about it and try to stop them? Both of those are only my favorite space alien movies, but that's okay.

Tina: Oh, you know what space alien movie everyone enjoys that's just like that? *E.T.*! How long has it been since you watched *E.T.*? In *E.T.*, a young alien falls to earth and some kids find him, but instead of attacking people, he's very sad and just wants to go home. Mia, do you think the twins are too young to watch *E.T.*?

Lilly: Oh, so we're on movies that kids would like now? Then definitely *Train to Busan* where a guy takes his young daughter to visit her mom on her birthday, but there's a zombie attack, so everyone on the train is getting killed, and the guy and his daughter have to battle zombies to stay alive. There's so much gore, it's *sick*.

Mia: That movie sounds *totally inappropriate* for young children. But if you like movies that take place on trains, then there is nothing better in the entire world than *Bodyguard* on Netflix, which starts out on a train. A British soldier with PTSD (SPOILER ALERT) saves everyone on the train and then becomes the VERY HOT bodyguard of the beautiful home secretary, who is trying hard to competently rule her country and then—

Tina: Oh my God, I saw that one! I will agree with you about *Bodyguard*, Mia. That was literally the best series— well, except for the violent bits, and the deaths. I wish they'd make *Bodyguard 2*

starring me as the girl who that guy has to
bodyguard.

Mia: Me, too! I mean—not really, I love
my husband, but—

Tina: And I love my boyfriend! But that
bodyguard—

Lilly: Okay, I like that bodyguard, too.
But I like pretty much anything with a
bodyguard in it—

Mia: Gee, I wonder why.

Lilly: Like *The Hitman's Bodyguard* with
Ryan Reynolds—

Tina: Oh, he's so cute! But he's not my
favorite Ryan. That would be Ryan Gosling.
I love anything with Ryan Gosling, except
of course for *La La Land*. I do not like the
ending of that movie at all.

Lilly: You're right. *La La Land* is probably
the most frightening movie of all. Aside
from *Children of Men*, based on the
dystopian P. D. James novel about life after
humans become infertile, in which Clive
Owen has to smuggle a refugee out of the
UK for mysterious reasons.

Mia: Oh, really? You think that's more frightening than Margaret Atwood's *The Handmaid's Tale*, in which women become literal slaves because of their reproductive ability?

Tina: My favorite show about women and their reproductive ability these days is *Call the Midwife*! I love watching BBC period dramas, and those midwives from the 1950s and 60s wear the best clothes . . . plus all the babies are so cute! And there are tons of sweet romances. But also diphtheria, of course, which is not so sweet or cute.

Lilly: Okay, fine, but can we all just agree that the best show is *Westworld*? It's no *Watchmen*, of course, but then what is?

Mia: Agreed. Michael loves both those shows. Michael loves—

Lilly: What *I* would really love right now is to have a conversation that is just between us women, that does not include any references to the men in our lives.

Mia: Why? What's wrong? Is there trouble in paradise between you and my bodyguard?

Lilly: No! I would just love, for once in our lives, to not have to listen to you go on and on about how great my brother is.

Mia: I don't do that! Do I do that?

Lilly: Yes, actually, you do.

Mia: Well, I can't help it. Your brother is very supportive of me and of *all* women, actually, so I'm not sure how you expect me to just ignore that. Right now, as a matter of fact, as he sits in total isolation, your brother is helping to work on a vaccine to prevent billions of women *and* men around the world from catching this terrible virus—

Lilly (sighing): Oh my God, *fine.* Forget about it. Go on, Tina.

Tina: Okay, well, what I'm really enjoying watching right now besides *Call the Midwife* is *Schitt's Creek.* It's so gentle and calming and very women positive and I cried at the sweetness of it. I want that show to be watched by everyone and win all the prizes.

Mia: Okay, Tina, your list wins.

Lilly: I'm a big enough person to agree
that it does.

Tina: Oh, thank you! Let's all watch *Emma*
together when we get a chance.

Mia: Done.

THREE MORE DAYS until Michael is out of self-isolation.

Quarantine Day 12
Royal Bedroom

Something good at last! We appear to have got into some kind of a routine here at the palace (at least most of us).

- Michael is working remotely from self-isolation with the international team he's assembled to come up with a vaccine. But not just any vaccine, one that is administered as a mist through the nasal passages. As he puts it, "The nasopharynx is the primary entry point for SARS-CoV-2, so targeting the nasal cavity could be one of the best lines of defense for vaccines." It's lovely to be married to someone who is so smart, even if half the time I don't understand a thing he says.

- The school finally got the "distance learning" program underway, and Olivia and Rocky have been at their computers all day, attending "class." Once we got all the

snags worked out—and there were a LOT.
I never thought I would have to use the
FOIL method again, but here it is, only they
don't call it that anymore, at least not in
Genovia—it has been blessed silence ever
since! For now.

• Mom's teaching the twins to finger paint.
  "They really are quite talented, Mia," she
  told me this afternoon. "Especially Frank.
  He might be another Banksy!" (**Note to
  self:** Not sure this is a good thing. Google
  Banksy later.)

• Even Dad has found a meaningful way to
  spend his time: he is over at the summer
  palace, supervising the construction crew
  there. Construction is considered an
  essential service, and residents are allowed
  to leave their homes for work purposes if
  they wear a mask. I'm counting supervision
  of a home renovation as work, even if the
  home is a castle. Interesting that all it took
  was a pandemic and being trapped at
  home all day with his extended family and
  no nannies or housekeepers to get Dad
  motivated to finish construction on his
  home.

• Lilly is working on the case that's been
  filed against me by the Genovian Hotel and

Restaurant Association for shutting down
the country. She says I'm a lock to win. I
really want to believe her.

• Grandmère is self-isolating on a lounge
chair on the far side of the pool, closest
to where Derek is living. She's wearing
nothing but a maillot and working
through her second case of wine. It's not
MY wine though and I can't hear her, so
I don't care.

All this has left me free to finally get back to
work!

Of course most of my work is focused on making sure the people of Genovia have what they
need during this critical time: money for food,
rent, medicine, and utility bills while their places
of work are closed; support for their mental
health needs (so vitally important, but so often
neglected); etc.

So I'm spending most of my time volunteer-
ing at Genovia Cares!, the nonprofit *I* started to
provide goods and services to the indigent and
underprivileged in this region.

But it turns out every single person my age
and older who doesn't have family to care for
or work to do at home right now is also showing up to volunteer at Genovia Cares!. In fact
we have more volunteers than we do people

seeking goods and services from Genovia Cares!.

So I was sent home, especially when a gaggle of paparazzi—rabid for feel-good stories during this dark time—showed up to photograph me slicing carrots for my nonprofit's healthy take-home boxed lunch. I was deemed by the chief coordinator to be a "distraction" and possible safety hazard.

So today I decided instead to tackle my mail.

After cracking open a bottle of pinot grigio (one should never approach the mail these days sober), I carefully donned rubber gloves, then wiped down each envelope with Clorox wipes before slitting it open with my healing quartz–encrusted letter opener (a wedding gift from Gwyneth Paltrow).

Then, still using my gloves and wearing my face mask (a Hermès scarf because of course we don't have any real face masks—they've all gone to the hospital for the doctors and nurses to use while examining patients), I began to read:

To Her Royal Highness, Princess Amelia
Mignonette Grimaldi Thermopolis Renaldo:

> *My parents were intending to throw me a graduation party at the Royal Genovian Yacht Club in May. Do you know if Genovia will still be shut down in May? If not, could you please*

open the country back up by May 19 so that I can have my graduation party?

If not, will you make sure that my parents receive a full refund of their $1500 deposit? I would like to use it on beauty products.

Yours very sincerely,
Ashley (last name withheld
for security reasons)

Ha! Why, no, Ashley, Genovia will not in any way be affected by COVID-19 in May. Just because Italy, the country next door to us, is the epicenter of the pandemic in Europe, there's no reason to think that there's any possibility that your graduation party should be affected.

I can understand her disappointment, but what are people thinking? I'm only a princess, not a fortune-teller! Not even epidemiologists who have been working in this field for years and years know when this pandemic is going to end.

But I will have my personal assistant, Sayeeda, write Ashley a polite reply informing her that a refund will be issued to her in the event that her party has to be canceled, and also send her a pear and olive oil gift basket as a token of my regret for her unfortunate circumstances.

Next:

Dear Cousin Mia,

It is I, Ivan, wondering if it is not time to put all of this silliness behind us. Yes, I know you are angry with me because I kept my many profitable bars open in secret after your lockdown order.

But I am a businessman. This is what I do! It is why I am so successful.

And as a businessman, I feel that it is my duty to inform you that NOW is the time to reopen the country. We have had only one positive case of the virus! Obviously we have beaten this terrible disease! It is a miracle.

Now do the right thing for all of Genovia, and REOPEN THE COUNTRY.

Yours truly,
Count Ivan Renaldo

Ha. HA HA HA HA!
I have to laugh, because if I don't, I'll cry.
A miracle! HA! It isn't a MIRACLE that we've only had one case of the virus. IT'S BECAUSE OF THE LOCKDOWN and everyone staying home and out of his "many profitable bars"!
Oh God.
I'm having Sayeeda craft a brief response, simply saying "no."

And he is NOT getting a gift basket.
Finally, this:

Dear Princess Mia,

*Hello. You do not know me. We have never
met. I am a mother who lives in America.*

*But I would like to thank you from the bot-
tom of my heart for the kindness that you have
shown my son, Chad (last name withheld for
security reasons). He is the COVID patient
currently hospitalized in your country.*

*I don't know how to express my gratitude
for the care you and the people of Genovia, particularly the doctors, nurses, and other hospital
workers there, have shown him.*

*Mostly, it has made me think that the term
"social distancing" is so grossly inaccurate.
Even though we are so very far away from
each other, I have never known such social
warmth.*

*I think that many of us in the last month
have experienced incredible "social" connection like we've never had before. From Zoom
business and social meetings to people simply picking up the phone and reaching out to
someone they haven't spoken to in a very long
time to people like you, who have shown such
kindness to a person you don't even know,
who isn't even a citizen of your country—
strangers simply being generous and support-*

ive to one another in a time of great personal
need.

Maybe the phrase shouldn't be "social distancing" at all, but "physical distancing," because that seems more accurate to me. We are
more warm and "social" than ever, while keeping
"physically" distant.

Words are important, and so are people. ONE
WORD, just like ONE PERSON, can change the
world . . . and you have changed ours for the better forever. Thank you, thank you, thank you for
physically distancing while not social distancing!

Sincerely,
Linda (last name withheld
for security reasons)

Aw! Chad's mom, Linda! I love her! I really do.
It's not the wine, either—I truly love her!

I'm going to have Sayeeda send Linda TEN
gift baskets (although it might be difficult to get
them through customs).

Maybe I should make her a duchess, instead?
Duchess Linda has a nice ring to it.

Because she's right: "physical distancing" sounds
much better—and is more accurate—than "social
distancing." It's what we're all doing, while staying
"socially" closer than ever.

I'm going to have my media team implement
it immediately into all of Genovia's coronavirus
messaging!

Oh—I hear the babies crying. Finger paint time must be over. More wine—I mean, more later!

TWO DAYS UNTIL Michael is free from quarantine jail!

Quarantine Day 13
Royal Bedroom

This morning I was on the phone with the chancellor of Germany, trying to get some coronavirus test strips (we cannot reopen the country until we've tested everyone, like my role model country, Iceland, which, in addition to having 100 percent literacy, has tested 100 percent of its residents), when Grandmère appeared in front of my desk with Derek, whom I've agreed to shelter here at the palace until the airport reopens and I can send him home.

I should have known something was up. Both Derek and my grandmother were smiling broadly.

Never in a million years, however, could I have guessed what was making them so happy.

"May I help you?" I asked, when I finished my call.

"Be the first to congratulate me," Grandmère said, and held out her hand.

On her left ring finger glittered the smallest diamond imaginable.

I'm sorry to say that my reaction was not at all princessy.

"*What?*" I cried, nearly falling out of my chair.

"That's right." Grandmère looked smug as she withdrew her hand to curl it around Derek's ample biceps—which were bare, by the way, because he was wearing board shorts and a tank top with the number 24 on it. "We're getting married. Sooner rather than later. I feel that the Genovian people need something to celebrate right now, don't you? And after a birth, a marriage is the most joyous celebration of all."

"The people need something to celebrate, all right," I said. "But it most definitely is *not* going to be your marriage to—" I stared at Derek. "Forgive me, but what is your last name?"

"Oh, no worries, it's cool," said Derek. "Zagorski. Derek Zagorski."

"Thank you. Well, one thing the people of Genovia most definitely do *not* need right now, Grandmère, is to celebrate your marriage to Mr. Zagorski."

"Oh?" Grandmère raised her drawn-on eyebrows to their limits. "And why is that, pray?"

"Because you've only known one another for two weeks!"

"*Three* weeks!" Grandmère cried, rolling the *r* in *three* as she is wont to do when being particularly dramatic about something.

"Fine, three weeks. How many marriages do

you know of that worked out well after a mere three weeks of acquaintance?"

"Lyle Lovett and Julia Roberts!"

"I don't think that's the best example." I looked at Derek. "Do you even know who Lyle Lovett and Julia Roberts are?"

Derek shook his shaggy head. I don't know if he wears his hair shoulder-length on purpose or because all the barbershops in Europe have been closed for so long. That can't possibly explain the beard, though. Obviously he wears that to cover his weak chin, but surely someone must have taught him how to shave.

"No," he said, happily. "Well, Lyle, bro, for sure. His music's real sweet. As for the Julie chick—no. But it's all good."

Of course it was "all good" . . . for Derek! He's a penniless student currently engaged to a dowager princess worth hundreds of millions of dollars (mostly in real estate and jewels, but still). Things were more than "all good" for Derek!

"Grandmère," I said, from between gritted teeth. "May I have a word with you in private?"

Grandmère bristled. "No, you may not—not if you're going to attempt to talk me out of marrying Derek. Because I won't be talked out of it, Amelia. I think it's a perfectly splendid idea. We've all been cooped up inside for months—"

Me: "Two weeks."

Grandmère: "—and a wedding is exactly what we all need to feel alive again! It's past time to reopen the country and allow the people to go back to their normal lives—most especially to plan for my royal wedding to Derek. People love planning for a festive occasion, and what is more festive than a wedding? I've already phoned Sebastiano to make up my gown—"

Me: "Sebastiano is in quarantine in the Hamptons. How is he going to make a wedding gown for you when he is 4,000 miles away?"

Grandmère: "Love always finds a way! Let the Royal Genovian Guard know that the beaches and parks are to be opened again so that the people can experience the freedom I feel in my heart—"

Me: "Nope."

Grandmère: "And of course all the shops and boutiques must reopen immediately so that the people can begin their wedding gift shopping—"

Me: "Absolutely not."

Grandmère: "And what's a wedding
without music? You must fly that what's-
his-name over to perform a live concert on
the beach in honor of my engagement—"

Me: "You don't mean Boris Pelkowski, do
you?"

Grandmère: "I do. Only Olivia and her
friends call him Boris P, now, I believe."

Olivia and her friends aren't the only ones. It
still irks me that Boris Pelkowski, the annoying
mouth-breather I went to high school with, who
spent hours every day scraping away at his violin, is now an international pop sensation. I guess
it's true what they say: practice makes perfect.

Or, in the case of Boris, one of the world's best-
selling recording artists, with sales of over 100
million records worldwide, but still no social
skills.

Grandmère: "And Derek will of course
be creating a spectacular playlist to go
with the fireworks display that you will be
setting off in my honor on the eve of our
nuptials—"

Me: "That will be happening over my dead
body. And yours, too."

Grandmère: "Of course we can have the groomsmen bring out the royal coach—"

Me: "The groomsmen have all left to be home with their families until the crisis is over."

Grandmère: "Well, the stable hands, then. And of course the casinos must be reopened. Can you believe that Derek has never played baccarat?"

Me: "I can believe that, and no, I won't be reopening the casinos anytime soon."

Grandmère: "Oh, and we must have wedding cake, Amelia. Something simple like the one you had at your wedding will suffice. Mine is a second marriage, anyway, so I wouldn't want to look as if I'm putting on airs. Just make sure that it's large enough to serve five hundred, because that's how many people I intend to invite to the reception."

Me: "Oh, really? That's all?"

Grandmère: "Well, I don't want to overdo it. People are suffering, you know. It would be boorish to appear too ostentatious in light of current world events. Oh, and

make sure they bring out all the best
champagne from the royal wine cellar. It's
the perfect way to say, 'The emergency is
over, everyone! Come out, come out, and
celebrate with us!'"

Me: "Sure, sure. But you do understand
that the emergency is *not* over, right?
There's still no cure or vaccine. We don't
even know whether people like Chad,
Derek's friend, who've had the virus, can
catch it again. I presume you'll want Chad
to attend?"

I directed this inquiry to Derek.

"Damn straight," he said. "Chad's my bro!"

"Yes," I said. "I'm sure he is your, er, bro. Well,
you see, that might pose a problem considering
he's still in the hospital."

"We can wait until he's out," Grandmère said,
with a dismissive wave of her hand. "I'm certain
it will only be for a few more days. That will give
us time to register for our gifts. And of course to
make arrangements for all of Derek's family to be
flown in from Dayton."

"Daytona," Derek corrected her. "Dayton is in
Ohio. I'm from Daytona, which is in Florida."

"Sorry, my mistake."

"Well," I said. "That might be a problem, as
well, given that the airport is still closed to both
domestic and international flights."

"Well, you must open it, Amelia. What are you thinking? It's for the good of the people!"

"Yes, I will take that under consideration," I said. "Can I just ask a personal question first, though?"

"Of course."

"Why *him*?" I smiled apologetically at the groom-to-be, who was stroking his beard while checking his text messages. "No offense, Derek."

"Oh, yo, no worries," he said, amiably.

"Thanks. I won't worry." To my grandmother I said, "Seriously, though. What is it about Mr. Zagorski that makes him dowager prince consort material?"

She blinked at me as if *I* were the crazy one. "How can you not see it, Amelia? He is my soul mate."

I'm sorry to say I snorted. I couldn't help it.

"Your soul mate? And what, precisely, do you and Derek, a nineteen-year-old student from the University of Florida, have in common?"

"Music," Grandmère said. "Derek and I share the deepest of loves for the language of song."

This was such complete and utter baloney. My grandmother had never in her life expressed a great love for music. Except for when she'd been in school and played Yum-Yum in *The Mikado*—a fact she would never let any of us forget, particularly by singing "Three Little Maids from School Are We" every morning before coming to the breakfast table, until my father established a "No Singing Before Breakfast" rule—she has never cared one jot for music.

Until now.

"Yeah," Derek said, finally looking up from his phone. "Your grandma has a dope record collection."

Oh, dear God.

"Yes," I said. "I'm sure she does." Some of Grandmère's records are, in fact, 78s, of which she takes abysmal care, even though they're quite rare. "But is that enough on which to build a foundation for a lifelong relationship?" Although in Grandmère's case it might be, because who knows how many years she's got left?

Then again, she smokes and drinks so much, she is basically pickled.

"Royals who have far less in common with their chosen spouses seem to have done fairly well in their marriages," Grandmère shot back. "Look at Prince Harry."

It was my turn to bristle. "How dare you!" She knows how I feel about my darling Harry and Meghan.

"Or you and Michael," she added, savagely.

I actually gasped. "Michael and I have tons in common!"

"Do you?" Her smile was venomous. "A celebrated scientific engineer and a . . . princess?"

I'm sorry to say I lost my temper then. "Stop it! You know what I'm talking about! Derek is nineteen and you're ninety, at least!"

Grandmère sucked in her breath as sharply

as if I'd slapped her. Derek, however, merely shrugged. "Hey," he said. "I don't care about age. It's only a number."

Grandmère, however, had saved her final, most brutal barb for last: "You are being ageist, Amelia," she said. "I never would have expected it from you, of all people. But there it is."

Ageist! I was not being ageist . . . was I? It didn't matter to me what age Derek was—or Grandmère either, for that matter. I would be against her marrying ANYONE she'd known for only three weeks.

And certainly suspicious of her motives, because she is not, in the words of Robert Browning, a woman whose heart is too soon made glad.

"But after all," Grandmère cried, taking Derek in her arms. "Love is love, is it not, my sweet?"

"Damn straight," Derek said, and then the two of them—ew, I can hardly write it here—kissed.

Right in front of me!

"Ugh," I said. "Fine."

Grandmère pried her lips off her groom-to-be long enough to ask, "Does that mean you're giving us your blessing, Amelia?"

Fortunately, I kept my cool. I said, in my most princessy tone, "Absolutely. Allow me to be the first to congratulate you on your forthcoming nuptials. As legal adults, you can apply for a marriage license at any time."

Grandmère and Derek both gasped with excitement, and hugged one another, and kissed some more. But I wasn't finished.

"But there isn't going to be any sort of wedding like the one you're describing . . . at least, not anytime soon. If your love is really as strong as you say, then you should be happy to wait for your five-hundred-person reception until it's safe for the country to reopen. In the meantime, if you can't wait, Derek's family can certainly be present at your nuptials via Zoom, and all of your family will be there for you, too, Grandmère . . . wearing face masks and seated six feet apart in the palace chapel where you two can be married at once by an online justice of the peace."

"But," Grandmère sputtered. "But . . . the only point was for us . . . to reopen the country—for the good of the people, of course—!"

"Exactly. And believe me, I'm doing *this* for the good of the people," I said. "And my own sanity. Have a lovely day."

Then I left—even though it was my own office—and went to find my dad to tell him that his mother has officially lost her mind.

ONLY ONE MORE day until Michael is out of self-isolation!

I found Dad in the media room desperately trying to find live sports to watch on satellite TV. He was flipping woefully between channels.

"Dad," I said. "Did you hear what your mother is planning on doing?"

"Marry a man half her age?" Dad found something that appeared to be Austrian summer tobogganing and settled on it glumly. "Yes, I'm aware."

"*Half* her age? Try a quarter, if that. Do you have any opinions on the matter?"

"What would it matter if I did, Mia?" Dad flipped grumpily to a French monster truck rally. "You know she never listens to me. She never listens to anybody."

"Yes," I said, remembering what Tina had said about the benefits of meditation and taking a deep, calming breath. "But we aren't actually going to let her go *through* with this thing, are we? She wants a royal wedding with fireworks and a five-hundred-person guest list and a dress by Sebastiano and champagne from the wine cellar and all of that. During a pandemic. But even if there wasn't a pandemic—"

"Mia." Dad finally switched off the TV in defeat and turned to face me. "You know this wedding is never going to happen. Your grandmother is going to get tired of this one and get rid of him, just like she has all the other men she's dated since your grandfather died."

I raised my eyebrows skeptically. "Uh, I wouldn't exactly call this one a man. More like a boy. And she never got engaged to any of those others."

Dad walked over to the liquor cabinet. "Your grandmother simply needs a distraction from the horror that's going on outside these palace walls, same as the rest of us. Let her plan her little wedding. I guarantee you it's not going to happen."

"But that's the problem, Dad. It's not a little wedding, it's huge. And let's say I agree with you that it's only a distraction—which I don't, necessarily—she's going to run up some pretty sizable bills, and maybe get her heart broken."

He glanced at me over the whiskey he was pouring. "You think my mother has a heart?"

"Dad!" Though he had a point.

"Trust me, Mia," he said with a grin as he handed me one of the whiskeys. "Your grandmother will be fine. The boy, however—what is his name?"

"You mean Derek, your future stepfather?"

"Yes, Derek. Derek, I wouldn't be so sure of."

"Why? Are you going to sic Lars on him?"

"Absolutely not. But I have a feeling your grandmother is going to put him through his paces."

I rolled my eyes. "All right, fine. But don't say I didn't warn you."

Dad raised his whiskey in a toast. "To Derek. God help him."

I clinked his glass with my own. "To Derek. My future grandpa."

ONLY TWELVE MORE hours until Michael is out of self-isolation!

Quarantine Day 14
Royal Bedroom

Today it finally happened:

Michael was released from self-isolation!

And thanks to my incredible skills in diplomacy (but mainly because I'm a female leader of a constitutional monarchy, and in this world health crisis, female leaders have so far shown the best responses, banding together like lionesses to keep our ~~pride~~ countries safe and healthy), I acquired eleven hundred rapid coronavirus test kits from the chancellor of Germany.

So Dr. Khan gave Michael one, and . . . he passed! He has been declared officially virus-free!

"Oh, Michael!" I cried, after he'd given the twins hugs and kisses, then walked into our bedroom, where I was finally able to throw my arms around him and inhale his fresh Michael smell. Instantly, I felt better than I had in days—fourteen days, to be exact.

I'll talk to him later about the beard he appears to be growing. And I don't understand what is going on with his sideburns.

But those are small, superficial things that don't matter compared to what is important: Michael is back in my arms!

"You won't even believe what happened while you were gone, Michael," I cried. "The Genovian Hotel and Restaurant Association is suing me for shutting down all the bars and casinos! And Lana tried to come visit for Easter! And Fat Louie has hyperthyroidism! And Rocky got into a fight with a swan! And Grandmère is engaged to a nineteen-year-old music history major from the University of Florida, and fully intends to marry him, despite their seventy-year-or-more age difference. And she accused me of being ageist!"

"Mia," Michael said, as he untied my sweatpants. Really I should have dressed up a little for his return, but I've stress eaten so many cookies that none of my regular clothes fit anymore. "I already know all that. I was in a guest room down the hall, not Siberia. You and I saw each other across the balcony every day, remember?"

"Oh, right." I believe I'm suffering from quarantine-induced amnesia. I can't remember what day it is or even what month. "Well, what are we going to do?"

"Maybe we could wait a day or two to figure it out." Michael pulled off my comfy knee-length quarantine cardigan and also the *I Heart Genovia* T-shirt I've been wearing for several days straight beneath it. I would have changed, but it's my only shirt that fits. "Hmmm, what's going on here—no bra?"

"Michael," I scoffed. "It's a pandemic. No one wears a bra anymore. Not unless they're jogging or giving a press brief—"

I didn't get to finish, however. That was because he'd thrown me across the bed, where we spent a very pleasant half hour or so ravaging each other's bodies.

His body hadn't changed so much since I'd last seen it (except for the beard and sideburns, which I honestly don't understand since he had to have had a razor in there. Unlike me, who has had no access to Paolo or hair dye, so I'm growing a white stripe down the part in my hair that looks exactly like the one the mom grew in the original *Poltergeist* movie after she entered the gate to the other dimension to rescue her daughter Carol Anne from the ghosts. Ruling a country during COVID is a lot like entering a gate to another dimension, just without the ectoplasm).

Of course, Michael wasn't left alone to cope with twin toddlers, a demented senior, and an entire country that's demanding to reopen even though there is no scientific data to indicate that this would be safe, so all that happened to him was that his facial hair got longer.

But when you're in love, looks don't matter, as we know from *Beauty and the Beast*. Even something as hideous as a beard and sideburns like a soldier from the Civil War can still be sexy . . . or at least politely ignored for the time being.

Afterward, when we were still snuggling together in the afterglow of amazing reunion sex, Michael said, "Would you care to tell me why there's a wine refrigerator next to the bed?"

"Oh," I said, lifting my head from his chest. "Because it's more convenient to have it here than in the closet, where it used to be."

"I think what I meant was, why is there a wine refrigerator in our bedroom *at all*?"

"Oh, well, because it was getting so inconvenient to keep asking the major domo to have wine bottles sent to my room. This way, all I have to do is lean over and grab one. I've gotten fast enough now that I can reach down and open a new bottle in the fifteen seconds between episodes of shows on Netflix without even missing the intro. Speaking of which, where are my manners? Would you like a glass? I have a very nice pinot gris from a case sent to me by the prime minister of New Zealand. They, by the way, are doing amazingly in their battle against COVID."

"Mia, it is eleven o'clock in the morning."

"Michael, this is Europe. People drink wine at lunch all the time."

"Since when is eleven o'clock lunch?"

"Michael, a lot of things have happened since you went into self-isolation, and I'm not just talking about my grandmother getting engaged to someone who isn't even old enough to remember MySpace. The world is different. We wear face masks and stand six feet away from one another—or at least we're supposed to. There are lunatics out there who insist that their civil rights are being violated by being asked to do so. Everyone else is trying to make the best of it, doing the socially responsible thing like staying home and helping their kids with distance learning, which is basically horrible for both the parents and the kids, and when this is over, I'm asking Parliament to give teachers huge raises. So we have all started drinking wine in the morning to cope, and no one judges anyone else for it."

Michael spread his hands wide. "I'm not judging! Obviously, you've been working hard and deserve as much wine as you want. I was just surprised to see a wine refrigerator where the night table used to be, that's all."

"Well, the nice thing about wine refrigerators is that they work perfectly well as night tables. You see how nicely the lamp fits on there? And my box of tissues and moisturizer? It's essential to keep moisturizer around these days because your hands get so chapped due to having to wash them all the time. I've had to stop wearing the engagement ring you got me because I got a rash under it from all the hand sanitizer I've been using . . . and also it doesn't fit my finger anymore due to my cookie consumption."

Michael lifted my hand to his lips. "I noticed.

I thought you weren't wearing it because you'd forgotten me."

"What?" I was shocked. "Never!"

He smiled. "That's good to know. All that moisturizing has left your hands nice and soft."

"You like that, do you?" I asked with a knowing smile.

His smile was just as knowing. "I like it *a lot*."

"Would you like me to do some more stuff to you with my nice, soft hands?"

"Your hands, and other things. Maybe you'd like me to do the same to you?"

"Yes, *please*."

Quarantine Day 15
Royal Bedroom

*A*ll I wanted was twenty-four hours. Just twenty-four hours alone with my husband without the country I rule falling apart. Was that too much to ask?

Apparently it was.

Because despite my best efforts (and those of the prime minister. I can't take full credit for the amazing job Genovia has done thus far, keeping our cases at a minimum), today we had protesters—*protesters!*—at the palace gates.

I was so angry when I found out—especially since I had just had my only time off in *days* from dealing with this pandemic: the loveliest twenty-four hours ever, enjoying the company of my husband, who'd been locked in self-isolation for two weeks. For *two weeks*, I'd not been able to hold or be held by Michael Moscovitz!

Then finally he'd been declared COVID-free by the royal physician, and we rushed into each other's arms (well, all right—we rushed into our bed, where we spent a very pleasant day and night. Thank God for Mom and Olivia agreeing to watch the twins).

And what do I emerge from my lovely time off with my royal consort to find?

People screaming and yelling outside the palace gates—not even wearing masks, let alone physically distancing from one another—holding the most annoying signs, with slogans that said, among other things:

WE DEMAND HAIRCUTS!
LET MY PEOPLE GOLF!
DON'T CANCEL MY YACHTING SEASON!
BE LIKE LIECHTENSTEIN!
WE HAVE THE RIGHT TO PLAY BACCARAT!
WE WANT WINE!

What is *wrong* with my citizens? We've had one—*one* case of the virus!—thanks to my restrictions.

And this is how they show their thanks?

And neither I nor the prime minister has ever deprived anyone of wine. As if! The people of Genovia can get all the wine they want! Wine shops are considered an essential business, and are all open.

Everyone simply has to stay home to drink their wine. Is that so much to ask of anyone?

Same with haircuts and baccarat. People can get all the haircuts and play all the baccarat they want—*at home.*

And honestly, what does it even matter anymore how anyone's hair looks? I went on *national television* with my gray roots showing and split ends everywhere. Nobody cared (with the possible exception of Paolo).

THIS IS A DEADLY PANDEMIC. GET OVER YOUR HAIR.

And I never forbade yachting. People can yacht to their heart's delight. They simply have to keep their yachts at least six feet apart from other people's yachts while at sea—no lashing yachts together and having giant yacht parties.

And they can't dock in a Genovian marina unless they can prove Genovian citizenship.

What is so unreasonable about that?

And don't even get me started on the golf thing. Obviously everyone will be able to play golf again when the golf course figures out how to fix the little cup hole thingies so people don't need to stick their entire hands in there to retrieve their balls and infect one another. That's the golf course's responsibility, NOT MINE.

And Liechtenstein? *Liechtenstein?* Please don't act like Liechtenstein is any better than we are. They have at least fifty more cases than we do!

And fine, so Liechtenstein didn't close its borders, and has fewer restrictions. Do you know what Liechtenstein *also* doesn't have?

BEACHES. Liechtenstein is a LANDLOCKED COUNTRY. Liechtenstein doesn't have pure white sand beaches, turquoise waters, and an extremely low rate of virus (only one case so far here in Genovia, remember, and no fatalities), making everyone in all of Europe want to go there, unlike GENOVIA!

But I'm sorry, our hospital is extremely small, so if everyone DID come here, and then got sick (which is going to happen if we reopen), we wouldn't have enough ICU beds or ventilators for them, let alone enough PPE, face masks, or hand sanitizer for our health-care workers!

I did the absolute right thing by closing our borders. THE RIGHT THING.

OMG, if they like Liechtenstein so much, WHY DON'T THEY JUST MOVE THERE?

At first I was completely furious (and a little bit hurt) that my people were turning against me. So much so that Lars, my bodyguard, noticed, and was moved to say, "The Royal Genovian Guard just received a large shipment of Kalashnikovs, Your Highness, in case a neighboring country decides to invade us and steal our toilet paper. Do you want us to use them instead on that riff-raff out there?"

"God, Lars, no!" I was horrified. "I don't want you to strafe my citizens with automatic rifle fire. They have a constitutionally protected right to protest."

Lars looked disappointed.

But then Lilly, peering out the windows of the Great Hall, said, "It's not actually all that many people, Mia. One of them has a megaphone. It's so quiet around here with the lockdown, even a few people sounds like a lot."

Derek said, "If you'd like, Your Highness, I can turn on the palace sound system and play something really loud to drown them out. Harry Styles has that new song out—'Watermelon Sugar.' It's really great. Want me to play that?"

"No, Derek," I said from between gritted teeth. "I do not want the protesters blasted in any way, either by bullets or with 'Watermelon Sugar' by Harry Styles. The latter would be rewarding them."

Am I the only sane person in my family?

Then Michael, who'd immediately gone online to do some fact-checking, said, "Mia, those protesters are being paid."

"What?" I couldn't believe it. "What do you mean, paid? Paid by who?"

"Whom," Grandmère swanned in to say. "And of course they are. You don't honestly think Genovians would stand outside their palace for hours on end holding signs when they could be inside, drinking homemade pear schnapps and watching reruns of the Genovian Grand Prix?"

"The protesters are being paid by your cousin Ivan, Mia," Michael said.

Then he showed me his phone, on which he'd pulled up an online post from an account belonging to Crazy Ivan's, the bar and restaurant chain belonging to my cousin, Count Ivan Renaldo.

IMPORTANT

═══════════

*Count Ivan Renaldo is arranging a protest
for tomorrow morning in front of the palace
gates to demand that Princess Mia and the
Prime Minister take down the roadblocks
into Genovia and allow bars, restaurants,
beaches, and hotels to open back up.*

We need our tourists!

*The Count will provide premade protest signs
and free beer to every person who shows up.
RSVP below if you're coming so we can make sure
to have a sign for you, and also enough beer.*

*Please wear face masks and maintain
good social distancing at all times during
this protest. This virus is deadly.*

Thank you!

"Oh my God!" I cried. "So Ivan *knows* how
contagious this virus is. He just doesn't care
and wants me to open the borders anyway!"

"Right, because it's going to help him make
more money, so he can buy another yacht."
Michael took his phone from me and began
scrolling through the comments beneath the
post. "Looks like only about twenty people

signed up. They seem very excited about the free beer."

"The Genovian government is paying everyone more than enough in unemployment and COVID stimulus money to buy all the beer they want," I cried.

"I hate to say it," Grandmère began.

"But I'm sure you're going to say it anyway," I muttered. I was right:

"But none of this would be happening if Derek and I were having the royal wedding I suggested to you the other day, Amelia. The hospitality workers would all be too busy preparing for my big day to protest our closed beaches and lack of tourism. And of course Genovian citizens would definitely prefer free champagne and wedding cake to free beer. And a wedding is such a glorious thing! It offers people something to hope for. It represents romance and a dream for the future."

"Yeah, no," I snapped. "That is not going to happen. We are not having a royal wedding during a pandemic, and particularly not the royal wedding of the ninetysomething Dowager Princess of Genovia to a nineteen-year-old student from the University of Florida."

"Do you see?" Grandmère asked Michael. "Do you see how hardened and bitter your wife has become? I was hoping she might sweeten up a little once you got out of quarantine, Michael, but apparently this is her personality now."

Michael gave Grandmère a deadly stare, which I felt looked all the more devastating with his new beard and mustache, along with his quite unreasonably large sideburns. He resembles some of the seventeenth-century Genovian princes from the paintings in the Hall of Portraits.

"My wife is doing fine," he said. "She has almost single-handedly saved this country from a deadly pandemic. So I suggest you speak to her with a little more respect, Clarisse."

OMG! He's even sexier now than he was before he went into quarantine!

And Grandmère did seem suitably cowed—at least for her. She waved at him dismissively with her left hand—but probably only so we'd all notice her engagement ring (Derek had purchased a tastefully small diamond for her, which was all he could afford on a student budget and was perfectly fine, but Grandmère immediately sold some of her Apple stock and upgraded for a gigantic one that made her look like Thanos from the Avengers movies) and flounced from the room.

"Well," she said. "I can see where I'm not wanted! Come along, Derek, let's go see who won the Grand Prix from 1957. I appear to have forgotten."

Derek frowned and said, "Sorry, bro," to Michael. "Gotta say, though—someone sent me a bootleg copy of 'Rock Throwing Arab Youths.' Those were some killer lyrics. Would love to hear some of Skinner Box's other songs sometime." Then he followed Grandmère out the door.

"He really isn't that bad," Michael said after they were gone, "except for the fact that he's obviously trying to make your grandmother into his sugar momma."

"Are you serious?" I felt as if my head was splitting in two from all the cries of "Be like Liechtenstein!" coming from the gates. "You only like him because he complimented your old band!"

"No." Michael looked defensive. "That's not the *only* reason I like him. Anyone who can put up with Clarisse for as many hours of the day as he does has to have some positive qualities."

"He doesn't. He's the worst!"

But of course Derek isn't really the worst. And he and Grandmère are the least of my problems now.

What am I going to do about Ivan and his beer-swilling cronies?

UGH, remember when life was normal and I got to read books for fun and the only thing I had to worry about was what I was going to wear to this or that charity ball?

NOTE TO SELF: In 1919, then president of the United States Woodrow Wilson came down with a near-fatal case of the Spanish flu while attending negotiations in Paris to peacefully end World War I.

Although he survived physically, according to

all who knew him, he was never the same psycho-logically. Neurological symptoms were common in those whose respiratory systems had been so aggressively attacked, particularly in younger people, since their immune systems were stronger and tended to overreact to the virus.

Yet the American president continued to lie to his people that there was nothing to fear from influenza.

I personally make it a point never to lie to my people. And look at the thanks I get for it!

$\mathcal{T}$he prime minister called. "I have good news and bad news," she said.

"Of course you do," I said. "Well, let's get it over with. What's the bad news?"

"You're being sued."

"I already know that," I said with a snort. "The Genovian Hotel and Restaurant Association is suing me for shutting down all of their businesses due to the virus—even though of course we're giving them full financial support." I looked at my fingernails, which, since I haven't seen Paolo in so long, had returned to their normal unsightly state. "What else is new?"

"No, this isn't about that lawsuit," Madame Dupris surprised me by replying. "This is a new one. This one is from a small family-run Genovian bakery."

"A bakery?" I was shocked. "But why would a *bakery* sue me? Bakeries are considered essential businesses. They've all been allowed to stay open!" And if anyone else has been eating bread the way I have lately, their sales have probably been brisk.

"That isn't why they're suing you. They're suing you because they say your closing the country to tourists is adversely affecting their business. They say that last year at this time, when the airports and roads to Genovia were open, they were making 1,600 percent more in sales of croissants and éclairs than they are now."

"Well, how can they blame me for *that*?" I exploded, startling Michael and the twins, who were building a pillow fort nearby. "I didn't cause COVID-19! I'm trying to *protect* Genovia from it! You'd think these bakers would show a little gratitude to me for FORBIDDING tourists from coming here and bringing it to all of us!"

"Yes, well, that does not seem to be the attitude of the Paninis."

"Wait a minute." I could not believe what I was hearing. "These people own a bakery and their last name is Panini?"

"It appears so."

"This has to be a joke." Paninis are basically my favorite kind of sandwich. I love paninis of every kind—mozzarella, brie, chocolate, eggplant, even chicken and ham now that I've given up vegetarianism—I could go on forever. "This lawsuit has to be some sort of cruel prank by the paparazzi just to torment me."

"It does not seem to be. Monsieur Panini says his family has owned a bakery here in Genovia for over six centuries, and it is only since you shut down the country that his business has suffered irreparable financial harm—"

"It's only since I shut down the country that COVID has existed!" I thundered. "And anyway, what about the Spanish flu? You can't tell me his business wasn't affected by that! Let's find my grandmother. She was probably around then, I bet she remembers this Monsieur Panini and his alleged bakery, she can probably tell us. Or maybe the Black Plague years. How well were his croissants selling then? Let's consult the royal tax ledgers! Did his ancestors sue my ancestors for shutting down the country during the plague?"

"Well, Genovia didn't have tourists during the plague," Madame Dupris said. "Do you still want to hear the good news?"

"What possible good news could there be?" I asked, as Michael got up from all the pillows the twins had buried him under and came to rub my shoulders, since he could tell I was having a very stressful day. But not even his strong, manly fingers could rub away my anxiety over the Panini situation. "The people of my country are suing to get me to open up again to tourists, the exact things that will bring more cases of the virus here, and you think there's *good* news?"

"Yes," the prime minister said. "This year's graduating class of the Royal Genovian Academy would like you to give their commencement address. Of course they're only having a cyber commencement due to the virus, but they'd be honored if—"

I stood up, inadvertently flinging away Michael's hands. "I'll do it!"

"Oh." Madame Dupris sounded surprised. "You will? To be quite honest, I thought you'd say no, since you already have so much on your plate. And I do think you should know that apparently you were not their first choice. They asked Harry Styles first, then Taylor Swift, but apparently neither was available."

"Of course. Still, I'm happy to do it."

"How wonderful. I'm sure the students will be pleased."

"Thanks. And do get back to me about the baker if there are any developments." Perhaps the Paninis made paninis. Maybe if I ordered paninis for the entire palace staff—and the hospital staff, to show them how much I appreciate what a good job they're doing—it would make the Paninis so happy, they would drop their lawsuit.

"I will," said the prime minister. "Of course." Then we said our goodbyes and hung up.

"What is it?" Michael asked. "What's going on?"

"Mommy, Mommy," cried the twins. "Help us build our fort!"

"Not now, darlings," I said. "Mommy has something very important to do for the good of the country. I'm writing a commencement speech," I told Michael. "The Royal Genovian Academy's graduating class has asked me."

"Oh," he said. "Well, that's great. Have you ever written a commencement speech before?"

"Not that I can remember. I've been asked, of course, many times, but I've always been so busy attending UN sessions and opening hospital wings and whatnot, I've never had a chance actually to give one."

But we live on a different planet now. The UN is open only to virtual sessions and while many new hospitals are opening up, they aren't wasting time with royal grand openings. They're too busy trying to save patients.

So what can I possibly say to this year's graduating class, heading out into such a vastly different world than it was a mere two months ago, much less than when I graduated high school so many years ago? The world seems to be on fire—in some places, literally.

What can I say to these graduates to give them hope and inspiration for the future when I can sometimes barely summon any for myself, and I'm a princess who lives in a palace in absolute privilege and luxury?

"Amelia!" Grandmère is pounding on the door to my bedroom. "Amelia, I need to speak to you. It's about my wedding to Derek. It's IM-PORTANT! Stop avoiding me, young lady. You're going to have to come out and talk to me about this sometime. Now, we've whittled down the guest list to merely two hundred in deference to social distancing. But we absolutely refuse to wear masks. It's unseemly! Whoever heard of a bride in a mask? And we absolutely MUST have Harry Styles as our live entertainment during the reception, but if he's not available, Derek says he'll settle for someone called Lil Nas X."

And how am I even supposed to think while stuck inside with all this joyful toddler prattle, a newly bearded prince consort, and a love-crazed dowager princess distracting me?

Think. I've got to think!

I don't even know how long it's been since I last wrote in this diary. All the days seem to be blending into one another, exactly like Dr. Muhammad warned that they would.

I can see that the last time I wrote was right before I gave my commencement address to this year's graduating class of the Royal Genovian Academy.

I'm mortified by how that turned out:

"The future is in your hands," I said. "We're counting on you. What happens next is up to you!"

God. What a stupid thing to say. What was I even *thinking*?

Why are adults always telling young people that the future is up to them when adults are the ones who messed up their future to begin with? It's like in *A Wrinkle in Time* (which I watched the other day because we finally got Disney+ to work in the home theater here at the palace. It is a nightmare to get streaming services when your walls are three feet thick, even if you're married to a computer genius), when Mrs. Whatsit or whoever was telling those kids that it's up to them to destroy the evil that's slowly been eating away at the universe.

I remember reading that book when I was a tween and loving it so much.

But now, as the adult ruler of a principality, I was like, *"WHAT?"*

(And also, what was Mrs. Whatsit thinking, letting those children fly around on the back of a centaur or whatever it was without wearing seat belts? That is *extremely* dangerous.)

Anyway, sending kids off to save the universe from evil is WAY TOO MUCH RESPONSIBILITY to put on a child. And also not fair: the children didn't create the evil. Adults did!

Why are we depending on children to clean up the gigantic messes we've left behind? Adults should not only clean up their own messes, they should fight the evil themselves!

And, even though I know this is fictional, look what happened in the Star Wars universe when they allowed a child to go off and train to fight evil.

And yes, I suppose some people (Tina) think what Kylo Ren had going on with Rey was very sexy, especially when he had her chained up in that reclining chair, and also when they kept popping in on one another mentally and seeing each other half naked.

But in reality that relationship was abusive.

And also, Kylo sliced his father in half with a lightsaber, after which I was done with that series forever, even though both Michael and Tina assure me that Kylo found redemption (and a sexy death scene with Rey) in the last movie.

That's why what I ought to have done in my commencement speech is apologize. I ought to have said, "I'm sorry, kids, for leaving you with all of our garbage to deal with."

And then I should have assured them that SOME world leaders (such as myself) are definitely trying to fix things . . . and even succeeding. Over the past twenty years, the proportion of people living in extreme poverty has been cut in half. More children worldwide have access to medicine and clean water than ever before. And more and more animals are being moved off the endangered species list.

But right now, I will admit other things aren't looking so good. Like when the prime minister called me this morning and said, "Your Highness, I'm afraid in light of the lawsuits brought about by the Paninis and the Genovian Hotel and Restaurant Association, we really do have to reopen."

Me: "What? No!"

Prime Minister: "It only makes sense, Your Highness, since in the entire country of Genovia, there have been no deaths from

COVID, and only a single positive case. And
Chad of the University of Florida is better
now, as you know."

Of course I know. Chad's been living in my
pool house with my grandmother's fiancé since
I closed down the borders. He has no way to
get home—not that he'd want to. What college
student wouldn't prefer to lounge around in
a Genovian palace's pool house with his best
friend, playing video games all day, rather than
return to his parents' house in the Midwest?

Me: "But the *reason* we've only had one
case is BECAUSE we closed the borders
and all of the hotels and restaurants!"

Prime Minister: "I know. And no one
is prouder of our accomplishment than I
am. But we simply don't have an excuse
anymore not to reopen. The economy is
suffering, Your Highness."

Me: "I realize that, but think of all the lives
we've saved!"

Prime Minister: "I know. But we've also
exhausted all the overtime we allocated
to pay the Gendarmerie to keep out non-
residents."

The Gendarmerie are our local police force. We do not have the same problems here with our police as the US has had with some of theirs because we give our police ample training and pay, and also don't depend on them to do the kind of work that ought properly to be done by social workers, mental health experts, and jobs and community outreach programs. All 515 members of our Gendarmerie are beloved by both our residents and tourists for their white, warm-weather-appropriate shorts and cheerful attitudes.

But I have to admit they've complained of feeling a lot less cheerful since being on land-and-sea border patrol. Instead of wanting to take photos with them for their Instagram accounts, tourists stopped at the border now hurl insults and even water bottles at them. I don't blame the poor officers for feeling stressed.

> **Me:** "If money's the problem, I'm completely willing to pay their overtime myself."
>
> **Prime Minister:** "Out of your personal savings? Your Highness, no. I won't hear of it."
>
> **Me:** "If it will save lives, I'll be happy to do it."

Prime Minister: "Think how it would look to the rest of the world! Like we can't afford to pay our own workers."

Me: "American athletes and celebrities are donating vast amounts of money to local hospitals there—"

Prime Minister: "Oh, well, everyone in the world knows how inadequate the American health-care system is."

Me: "What if I were to sell some of the crown jewels, instead? It's ridiculous to have so many tiaras when people around the globe are literally starving."

Prime Minister: "Your Highness, you can't. Technically, those tiaras belong to the people of Genovia."

Me: "I know, but I think the people of Genovia would prefer being COVID-free to me having an assortment of tiaras to choose from to wear to formal events. And that diamond-and-drop-pearl one from Cartier that Grandpère gave Grandmère back in the fifties isn't even in style anymore."

Prime Minister: "It's out of the question.

Could you imagine what your grandmother
would say?"

Me: "She's remarrying anyway. I doubt
she'd even care."

I wasn't actually so sure about this. *Was*
Grandmère as in love with "Derek of Daytona" as she was claiming, or was her entire
engagement some sort of elaborate scheme to
get attention? (As a classic narcissist, there was
nothing Grandmère craved more. Negative or
positive, all attention was good, as far as she
was concerned.)

Or was Dad right, and she was simply trying to keep everyone's spirits up (including her
own) by planning a wedding during what was
one of the darkest periods in Genovia's history?

Seeing how she reacts to my selling an old
tiara of hers (though it did indeed technically
belong to the public now) might be an extreme
way to find out what she was really up to, but if
it worked, it might be worth it.

Except that the prime minister wouldn't play
ball.

Prime Minister: "Your Highness, I simply
won't allow it. Reopening is the only way.
The American Independence Day weekend
is right around the corner. That's when

many of our local businesses make the
most of their summer income, from US
residents traveling abroad."

I didn't have the heart to remind her that all
US residents had been banned from entering the
EU due to their astonishingly high infection levels, so it was unlikely our local businesses would
see an increase in income from tourists on the
Fourth or any other day of July. The prime minister had a lot on her mind, so it wasn't surprising
she'd forgotten this.

Prime Minister: "We have no choice.
We *must* reopen. The livelihoods of the
people of Genovia are depending on us.
We must think of this as a *good* thing, Your
Highness. We've won. We've beaten the
virus!"

Me: "Um . . . I'm pretty sure that's not
necessarily true. But if you really feel that
we ought to reopen the borders, I will of
course support your decision."

Prime Minister: "Thank you, Your
Highness."

Me: "Of course. I'm sure everything is
going to be fine."

I had to say that last part, even though I didn't actually believe it. The truth is that, like Princess Leia says in *The Empire Strikes Back*—the best Star Wars movie—just before the mynocks swoop in to attack, "I have a very bad feeling about this."

Quarantine Day ?????
Royal Bedroom

Grandmère always warned me that it's rude to say, "I told you so." No one appreciates it, and it only serves to "self-aggrandize, which is unattractive."

But I *knew* that as soon as we lifted the roadblocks at the borders, we were going to see a surge.

I said this to *everyone*, including Michael, who replied, "Mia, I get it. You said that five times during this episode of *The Mandalorian* alone, and I agreed with you every time. Now please can we unpause it to see if the Mandalorian saves that adorable alien baby?"

(*The Mandalorian* obviously doesn't count as part of the Star Wars series because it was not written by George Lucas and therefore is not canon.)

But did anyone listen to me? (Except of course for Michael, but he has to listen to me because we sleep together.)

No. Of course not!

"You're not a doctor," Grandmère said (because of course she wanted to reopen right away, in order to have her ridiculously large wedding).

"You're just a privileged princess," my cousin Ivan said (over the phone, because of course I don't allow him into the palace). "What do you even know about these things?"

They're both right. I'm not a doctor, and I *am* a princess. I have more privilege than anyone.

But I *have* seen (almost) every pandemic movie ever made. I have (almost) finished reading the longest book on Spanish flu ever written. I'm on WebMD all day long looking up diseases that I (or Michael or the twins or my siblings or parents) might possibly have.

I know how these things work.

And, perhaps more importantly, I know Genovia.

OF COURSE if you've been stuck in Italy or France or especially landlocked Liechtenstein during this difficult time, you're going to make a beeline for Genovia as soon as it opens its borders. Why wouldn't you? Because of our beautiful beaches, amazing food, gorgeous gardens, entertaining lounge acts, and of course plentiful liquor, Genovia is the *ideal* place to unwind after months of lockdown. We really do have everything.

So OF COURSE the second we opened, our

hotels and Airbnbs and even our parking lots (yes. People from Germany rode here in RVs) went from 0 percent occupancy to *114 percent occupancy.*

(I'll be honest with you, I don't understand where the extra 14 percent came from. How can something be 114 percent? I would ask Michael but I'm afraid he'd tell me, and as much as I adore him, his explanations can be a little long-winded, like John M. Barry's about the history of American medical colleges.

Michael's STILL trying to tell me about the nasal vaccine for COVID that he and his team are working on, and I honestly don't want to know until it's finished and we can start administering it, so I think I'll just remain in the dark about the mystery of the 114 percent.)

So anyway, right now our bars, restaurants, and beaches are PACKED with foreigners, most of whom refuse to wear masks because:

1. They insist they don't have to because they take vitamins and their "immune systems are healthy."

2. They don't want their "rights to be infringed upon."

3. "Masks are uncomfortable."

Even someone who hasn't watched the movie

Contagion fourteen times like I have could have predicted what happened next:

Suddenly bartenders, croupiers, Jet Ski tour operators, and servers at bars, casinos, hotels, and restaurants all around Genovia have begun experiencing symptoms of, then testing positive for, COVID-19.

Within just a few weeks, our numbers went from *one* (recovered) case to 1,024 positive and rising. We had *fifteen positive cases* in a single bar just today!

And despite what SOME people might think, I am NOT happy that the bar happens to belong to my cousin Count Ivan Renaldo.

I'm *definitely* not happy that Ivan himself is one of the people who tested positive. I would never be happy to hear that anyone has contracted a potentially fatal illness (or that his symptoms are apparently mild so far).

Nor was I happy when Tina phoned me urgently to say, "Mia, I saw on the news what's happening in Genovia. I hope you and Michael and the children are in lockdown at the palace!"

(We are, of course. I'm not even trying to go volunteer at Genovia Cares!. Now that we have Disney+, we've watched all of *The Mandalorian* and are about halfway through all movies in the Marvel Universe—only Michael and Rocky and Olivia and I, of course, the twins aren't watching those—and just about everything else on there, especially *Hamilton*, which I have now seen seventeen times, excluding live performances, but of course only the first act because the second act is far too sad, especially during a global pandemic.)

When a *doctor* calls you from NEW YORK CITY because they are concerned about the lack of social distancing and mask wearing in your country, you know the *merde* really has hit the fan.

"I'm not going to say I told you so," I said to the prime minister just now when I called her. "Instead, I'm only going to say that we've got to do something,"

"But what?" she cried. "We can't shut down again. The Genovian Hotel and Restaurant Association would never stand for it. Even though cases are up, so is the economy. The average daily rate for a hotel room right now is sixteen hundred euros a night."

Sixteen hundred euros a night? That is the equivalent of four orchestra seats to *Hamilton* on Broadway (if any shows on Broadway were even open, which they are not due to the highly contagious nature of COVID-19 indoors).

"That's fine," I said. "The borders can stay open. I have another idea."

"What are you going to do, Princess?" Madame Dupris sounded uneasy.

"You'll see."

Then I issued the following proclamation:

From Her Royal Highness Princess Amelia Mignonette Thermopolis Renaldo of Genovia

In view of the recent rapid increase of COVID-19 cases, the Genovian government in conjunction with the Royal Palace has declared that the wearing of masks is now mandatory in all public areas (indoors as well as outdoors).

Failure to wear a mask in Genovia will result in a 500 Euro fine and/or a minimum of three (3) days in jail.

***

"What if I have a healthy immune system? Must I wear a mask?"
Yes. The purpose of masks is to protect others who might have a more vulnerable immune system than you do.

"But aren't my rights being infringed upon?"

No. When you do not wear a mask in public, you are infringing upon the rights of others. If you do not want to wear a mask, please stay in your own home.

"My doctor says I don't have to wear a mask/I have a note from my doctor saying I do not have to wear a mask."
Notes from doctors saying you do not have to wear a mask in public are not valid in Genovia.

If doctors and nurses are able to breathe in masks for twelve hours a day during shifts treating COVID patients, surely you can breathe in yours for the few minutes it takes to consult with your sommelier over the type of wine you're ordering with your meal/walk down the street to get to your limo/try on clothes at Prada.

If you cannot follow the rules above, go somewhere that isn't Genovia.

If you need a mask, please contact the Royal Genovian Guard.

They are distributing them for free.

If you feel that you are experiencing symptoms of COVID-19, contact your physician. Do not go to the Royal Genovian Hospital or call emergency *services, which are currently overwhelmed. Your doctor will direct you how to proceed.*

Thank you for your cooperation.

—*Her Royal Highness, The Princess of Genovia*

I THINK THIS is quite fair. I can't imagine anyone disagreeing with any of it.

Quarantine Day Who Knows?
Royal Bedroom

I was wrong. It turns out there are some people who disagree with my mask mandate. One of them is in my own family.

I found that out this morning when I woke to a pounding on my bedroom door (at a very inconvenient time, I should add, as I was about to receive a pounding of a very different kind, since Michael and I were pretending that he was the chief fire inspector and I was a new homeowner who'd failed the Genovian safety standard codes by not installing smoke detectors).

But any plans of that nature were quickly abandoned when I heard Lars calling from the hallway outside my bedroom door: "Your Highness, it's me. We have an emergency!"

Obviously I thought something terrible had happened, like one of the twins had fallen out the window (even though I installed window guards that only allow them to open two inches), or got hold of a cell phone and somehow managed to dial NATO and order the carpet bombing of Libya.

But instead when I threw open the door, Lars said, "It's about your cousin."

At first I was relieved. "Oh, you mean Ivan? Yes, I know, he was admitted to the hospital last night. It's a shame, but I don't know what he was expecting, spending all that time inside his club without a mask, and with so many bachelor and bachelorette parties going on."

"Not that cousin." Lars handed me a pair of binoculars. "Go to the window and look down at the palace gates, Your Highness."

I did, and saw something that shouldn't have surprised me too much.

Except that it did.

Because there, dressed in jeans, a red plaid shirt, and a baseball hat with *Free Genovia* written on it, was my other Italian cousin, Prince René, shouting into a megaphone at a group of people who, at first glance, didn't look that much different than the ones who'd attended Cousin Ivan's protest.

Then, as I looked closer, I saw that these people seemed much angrier, weren't drinking any beer, and were holding very different signs:

MASKS ARE FOR CLOWNS!
MUZZLE MIA!
MY FACE = MY CHOICE!
GENOVIANS FOR TRUTH!
SOCIAL DISTANCING IS UNNATURAL!
DON'T LET THE TIARA TRACK YOU!
STAND UP TO ROYAL TYRANNY NOW!

Not only that, but a few of them, including René, were holding rifles. Granted, they were competitive target rifles made exclusively for shooting clay pigeons.

Still, they could definitely put someone's eye out . . . even if it would most likely be one of their own.

"What on earth do they hope to accomplish with this?" I asked, lowering the binoculars.

"I believe their intended goal," Lars said, "is to arrest you and the prime minister for crimes against the state."

I couldn't help it; I burst out laughing.

Lars frowned. "I'm glad you find it funny, Your Highness. They, on the other hand, seem quite serious."

"Oh, please," I said, passing the binoculars to Michael. "Arrest me for what? Because I issued a mandate for the good of the public health?"

"Why haven't *they* been arrested?" Michael demanded. Like Lars, he wasn't laughing.

"Arrested for what?" Lars asked. "They have the right under the Genovian constitution to assemble and protest."

"But they're holding *guns* outside the Royal Palace!"

"Firearms can be carried legally in this country as long as they're registered with and kept in the Genovian Hunting Club," Lars replied, though he didn't sound too happy about it. "And the owners have taken a six-hour-long firearms safety class, passed a weapons aptitude test, and have no history of mental illness or arrests for violence with the Genovian Gendarmerie."

I knew this law well, because I, along with the prime minister, had worked long hours to help to create it.

"But carrying them out in the open like that?" Michael exclaimed. "While also holding signs threatening to muzzle their royal princess?"

"That's why I woke you," Lars said. "I've already put the rest of the guard on high alert. Firearms must be kept on gun club property at all times, and even then may only be checked out of their safety lockers for no longer than four hours at a time. While none of these individuals are violating that policy—they haven't been there long enough—we intend to take them into custody the second they do."

"Hold on." I was already heading toward my dressing room, trying to figure out what my cousin could possibly be thinking. Normally in the summertime René could be counted on to do one thing and one thing only: show up poolside in a thousand-dollar Versace cabana suit with a tall Campari and soda in his hand. So everything happening down at those gates was totally out of character. "Before we start arresting people, let me go down and *talk* to René. I'm sure I'll be able to straighten this whole thing out without us having to make any—"

"*No!*"

It was quite astonishing to see two such large

men move so quickly, especially considering the fact that one of them was dressed in only a pair of drawstring pajama bottoms with penguins printed on them (Michael, obviously, not Lars).

"That isn't advisable, Princess," Lars said. "Like I said, they want to *arrest* you. The sight of you will only inflame the protesters even more."

"Oh my God," I said, rolling my eyes. "You two need to calm down. It's *René*. You remember *René*, who last time he visited the palace wouldn't eat solid foods because he and his wife were on a thirty-day juice cleanse? He obviously doesn't *really* mean to hurt me, any more than he really believes in not wearing masks. He's probably only doing this for the press because he's thinking of running for public office, or maybe he's starting a new line of rugged sportswear. He's a perfectly reasonable human being—"

"Except for when he's trying to steal your throne," Michael reminded me.

"Oh," I said. "Right."

You would think that by now I'd remember that I don't exactly have a normal life, and that numerous relatives (and ex-boyfriends) of mine have tried to stab me in the back just so that they, too, could have a slice of my (so-called) fame, fortune, and throne.

But somehow I always manage to forget. I'm certain Lilly would say it's because I'm subconsciously repressing these memories because they're so painful, and she would be absolutely right. She really ought to have been a shrink, like her parents, instead of a lawyer.

But then she'd have to pretend to be interested in other people's problems, and I know how much she'd hate that.

"Okay," I said. "Well, maybe I'll just give the prime minister a call."

"Good idea," Michael said, shooting Lars a look of relief I'm sure he didn't think I saw. But I did.

Honestly, I'm perfectly capable of running this country without the help of any man.

But I suppose it is nice to have them around, especially when it comes to emergencies—the pretend fire safety code kind, as well as real ones.

*J*ust got off the phone with the prime minister. She already knew about René and the rest of the protesters because news vans have begun showing up to report on them.

"Just ignore them," she said.

"Oh, I will," I assured her. "I never respond to negative reporting about Genovia."

"No, no," Madame Dupris said. "I meant your cousin and his merry band of idiots. It's best to let them get this out of their system, and then hopefully when they see how dismissively they're being portrayed by the media, they'll go home, the way your cousin Ivan did with his protest."

"Um," I said. "I think this might be a little different. Ivan is a calculating businessman who was paying his employees to protest. René is calculating, too, but in a different way."

I didn't want to remind her of the time René broke into the 1,400-year-old tomb of my ancestress Princess Rosagunde hoping to extract her

DNA and match it to his son, Morgan, in order to prove that Morgan was a more fit heir to the throne than I am, because it was so embarrassing to have a relative who would do something like that. But fortunately, I didn't have to, since she remembered.

"Yes," Madame Dupris said with a sigh. "That's true. But Prince René has never before shown himself to be violent."

"No," I admitted. "He hasn't. But we can't be sure about the other people in his group."

"Never fear. I'm having them scanned with the very best facial recognition software in the business. We should know by this afternoon if there's something in any of their backgrounds to cause concern."

I shouldn't have been as shocked as I was. "Genovia has facial recognition software?"

"With all of our high-end casinos and jewelry stores? Of course. We've stopped many a planned heist using it. Your cousin and his little friends will be watched around the clock by undercover police as well as surveillance cameras and satellite drones. You and your family will be completely safe. It isn't as if you aren't living in a medieval castle, after all, built to withstand attack from marauding invaders."

"Ha, ha." I pretended to find her little joke hilarious.

"But honestly," I went on, "I really do think we ought to meet with them—or at least René—and find out what they want."

"I think it's fairly obvious what they want, Your Highness. Their signs say so."

"Well, yes, of course. But couldn't we meet with them to explain why we don't intend to lift the mask mandate?"

The prime minister snorted. "I think that would be a waste of our time and the guard's resources. And I wouldn't want to give them a forum to spout their nonsense."

"But it might be a teachable moment." Ever since I'd learned the phrase "teachable moment," I loved using it. Even more, I loved seizing them, although unfortunately, since I have bodyguards, most of my teachable moments had to be planned rather than spontaneous. "An opportunity for us to offer them insight that they might otherwise never consider—"

"I won't have your safety—or, to be honest, mine—jeopardized, nor dignify their barbaric behavior with a response, even for the sake of a teachable moment. I'm sorry, Your Highness. I know he's your cousin. But I simply won't allow it."

"Yes," I said, with a sigh. "I understand."

But I wasn't sure I did.

The thing is, you can lock yourself behind all the fortified walls you want, but that doesn't keep you from feeling hurt when someone—someone you thought was family, much less a friend—betrays your trust.

I hate to admit it, but sometimes I wonder why we let anyone beyond our palace walls at all.

*O*f course no one can talk about anything other than what's happening down at the gates.

I don't mean just on Genovia 1, our own twenty-four-hour news (and entertainment) network. I mean in my own family.

"What's René up to this time?" my mother wants to know. "He can't possibly think wearing masks is a bad idea. He's such a germaphobe, he won't even allow his poor little son to play in the waves at the beach. He thinks ocean water might contain harmful bacteria."

I didn't say anything. René may not actually be wrong on this point. I've seen some of the results from water samples taken from beaches neighboring Genovia's and they are . . . not good. Unless you're a fan of enterococcus, that is. Why is it that we can keep our wastewater from running into our bay but other countries can't?

"I think we all know what your cousin René is after." Grandmère's sitting beside Derek, feeding

Rommel bits of hard-boiled egg from her salade niçoise. She isn't even bothering to sneak them to him, the way I occasionally sneak food from the table to Fat Louie. Rommel's sitting on her lap, enjoying food straight from the plate in front of her. Of course no one is saying anything to her about it, because who would dare? "What he's always after: the throne to Genovia."

"Well, he's not going to get it." I'm attacking my lunch, which is steak frites. The healthy-eating lifestyle Dr. Khan has encouraged me to follow in order to lose the baby weight went out the window with the pandemic, along with my public appearances—except for the regular televised updates to the Genovian people that the prime minister and I are giving, to reassure them that all is well in our battle against the virus, of course, and that the vaccine we're pouring so much time and money into will be ready soon.

But I've made sure that those updates are all shot from the shoulders up, at a flattering angle that doesn't show my new double chin.

Not that I'm not body positive. I completely am!

It's just that RateTheRoyals is not, and is forever comparing my body unflatteringly to Kate Middleton's. I have no idea what Kate eats, but apparently it isn't steak frites smothered in mayonnaise and ketchup—at least, not at lunch every day.

"René is lucky Genovia doesn't have the death penalty anymore," Lilly said. "I've been reading up on it, and under your grandfather's rule, what he's doing could have been considered an act of treason, punishable by execution."

Grandmère snorted. "Oh, please. Amelia's grandfather never had anyone executed, and most certainly not for treason."

Dad looked up from the sports section of the paper (not that there are any professional sports to report on. Instead, they're running "spotlights" on Genovian high school athletes and their pandemic training schedules and diets, none of which include steak frites). "Didn't Father once shoot someone for poaching at Miragnac?"

Grandmère raised her painted-on eyebrows. "That's different. He shot a hunter who trespassed onto the grounds of the summer palace and fired at Reginald, our favorite buck. Fortunately, the hunter missed. Your father didn't, though. That hunter walked with a limp for weeks."

"Really?" Rocky looked thrilled. "Can I have a gun like Grandpère? Then I can help defend the palace from all these people who hate Mia."

"Absolutely not." My mother's tone was brisk. "We have the Royal Genovian Guard to defend the palace from the people who hate your sister."

"No one hates your sister." I'm grateful that Michael, at least, came to my defense, since no one else in my family seemed interested in doing so. "Some people are afraid of change, and having to wear a mask to protect themselves and their loved ones from a deadly virus is a big change."

"I don't understand why anyone would be afraid of that," Olivia said. "Masks have been scientifically proven to save lives. Medical professionals have been wearing them for a hundred years or more to stop the spread of infection, and they've worked fine. How can those people—and Cousin René—not see that?"

"Yeah, about that." Derek looked confused, which was pretty much his normal expression. "How many cousins do you actually have, anyway, Your Highness?"

"She has only one first cousin," Grandmère informed Derek, in the sickly sweet voice she reserves only for him, and of course her beloved Rommel, Rocky, Olivia, and great-grandchildren. "Hank Thermopolis, her mother's sister's child. He lives in New York City where he had quite a successful career as a model, and where he's now also launched his own highly profitable line of men's undergarments. But all the rest are second and third cousins from my side of the family. I had just the one child, as you know—my precious Phillipe—due to my hostile uterus. And of course my sisters chose to devote their lives to doing good works instead of marrying."

Ha! Grandmère's uterus is probably the least hostile part of her. And doing good works? That's not exactly what I'd call what her sisters devoted their lives to. More like smoking, drinking, and talking bad about other people behind their backs—a lot like Grandmère, actually.

I could tell my mom was thinking along the same lines as I was because she said, not quite under her breath enough, "Funny how I've never seen Jean-Marie and Simone perform a single act of charity in my life."

"What was that, Helen?" Grandmère asked, only this time her tone was slightly laced with venom.

Mom raised her voice. "I said, funny how all of Mia's cousins except my sister's son, Hank, seem to think they have some kind of claim to the throne."

"It *is* strange." Grandmère took a sip of her champagne, which she now has at every meal because (she says) we're living through the apocalypse, so every bite could be her last, and she might as well enjoy it fully. I think I've shown admirable restraint in refraining from pointing out to Grandmère that she was doing this well before the pandemic started. "I suppose because their mothers, unlike me, raised their sons with a sense of entitlement. My parenting style was quite different. I held Phillipe to much higher standards. I never rescued him from his mistakes, or made him the center of my universe."

Mom just had a very long coughing fit. Dad had to smack her on the back a few times.

"No," Grandmère droned on, lost in her little fantasy about what a great mother she was. "I made sure that Phillipe always understood that even though he was a prince, if he wanted something, he had to *earn* it through hard work. I can't tell you how many times I found him out in the orchards, picking fruit with the other village boys, all so that he could earn a few centimes to buy his own sweets in town instead of asking his father for pocket money—"

This statement caused my dad to have his own coughing fit. I know as well as he does that everything Grandmère was saying was untrue—Dad's never done any sort of manual labor in his life, and in fact was shuffled off to boarding school almost as soon as he was potty-trained. But Derek and his friend Chad were both looking very impressed.

"Whoa," Chad said. "You really put a lot of thought into raising your kid, Clarisse."

"I did, Chadwick," Grandmère said. "Because I knew he wasn't going to grow up to be just anyone, but a world leader."

"It's just Chad," said Chad.

"Is there any more champagne?" Grandmère asked the footperson, ignoring Chad. "And may we have a rosé this time? I'm feeling festive."

"Of course, Your Highness," said the footperson with a bow.

"What was I saying?" Grandmère turned back to the table. "Oh, yes! Your father—"

I shudder to think how long this conversation would have gone on in this vein if Olivia hadn't (politely) interrupted.

"I'm sorry," she said. "But I still don't understand why those people are protesting Mia's mask mandate when they know it's to keep them from getting sick."

"Because they see Mia's mask mandate as an infringement on their personal freedom," Dad explained.

"But *speed limits* are an infringement on people's personal freedom," Olivia said. "So are building codes and sanitation laws. I don't see anybody protesting those."

"Spend enough time at City Hall and you will, believe me," crowed Lilly. "Kooks show up there every single day trying to get out of those, as well as out of paying their taxes, even though they still want their garbage picked up once a week, and their toilet water to go into the sewer—both of which are paid for by taxes, by the way."

"But we need all of those things," Olivia cried, "if we want to live together in a civilized society! They're for the good of the public, to protect the safety and health of the community. If we didn't have laws like that, people would go around hitting one another with their cars and leaving garbage all over the place."

My mother shook her head. "Just like Indiana in the seventies." Then she shuddered at the memory.

"The great John Stuart Mill wrote that liberty means doing what one desires . . . but only so long as one doesn't make a nuisance of oneself to others." Lilly had that faraway look in her eye she sometimes gets when she's reciting a quote she remembers—not from law school, but from her days as the teenaged hostess of a cable access television show.

Rocky asked, "Like you mean how Ivan didn't want to close his club and now he's given a lot of people COVID?"

"*Exactly*, Rock," I said, wondering how Grand-mère would respond to this, seeing as how she was pushing for a superspreader wedding.

But her only reaction was to exclaim, "I don't know *what* you're all so worried about, when this whole thing is going to be over by next month."

"What is?" I asked, startled. "This armed coup attempt by René, or the pandemic?"

"The pandemic, of course. I read online that this warm weather is eventually going to kill the virus, just like *that*." She snapped her beautifully manicured fingers, because of course she's still having her manicurist come to the palace to file and paint her nails.

"Really?" I couldn't believe my ears. "So explain why some of the warmest places on earth have such high rates of infected people."

"Oh, well," she said. "That's because it's peaked. But soon it's simply going to disappear."

"Sure," I said, exchanging an amused glance with Michael. "And you know this how?"

"Experience, Amelia. That's what happened

during the Spanish influenza, and that's what's going to happen with this one."

"Uh," I said. I still haven't finished John M. Barry's book, *The Great Influenza*, but I am on page 346, so I have a pretty good idea on how it all turns out. "That is *not* what happened during the Spanish influenza at all. There were multiple waves of variants of the virus, some more fatal than others, for several years until it finally mutated to the less deadly seasonal flu that millions of people still catch now every year, and lots of people even die from, unless they get a flu shot."

"Exactly what I said." She scooped Rommel into her arms, then rose with queenly grace to her feet. "Now if you will excuse us, Derek and I must go. Emile from Jewels of Genovia is bringing over a tray of wedding rings for us to choose from for our nuptials."

"Yeah." Derek snagged one last croissant from the basket in the center of the table. "Emile's got a special collection of wedding bands for men made from actual dinosaur bone fragments. They're called the Velociraptors. Is that sick or what?"

Chad and Rocky were the only ones who agreed that Derek's dinosaur bone ring was, indeed, sick, for which Grandmère and Derek thanked them. And with that, they sailed from the terrace.

I looked at Lilly and asked, "Legally, can I let

René have my throne if it means I don't have to deal with my grandmother anymore?"

She shook her head. "Extant royal primo-geniture-styled principalities don't work that way."

I checked on Wikipedia, and sadly, she's right.

Since I'd finished my weekly Zoom meeting with the United Nations Girls' Education Initiative (pervasive gender inequality as well as increased poverty due to the pandemic and/or political or environmental crises in their native lands are preventing millions of girls around the world from completing their education, causing many of them instead to be forced into marriage and even give birth at far too young an age), and I'm still not allowed out of the palace due to the "Stand for Face Freedom" protesters outside, I had nothing to do except play Candyland with the twins for the ninety-billionth time . . .

. . . as much as you *can* play Candyland with two-year-olds, since they don't really understand the game and so cheat (adorably but compulsively).

So that's what I was doing when the major domo knocked and said, looking unusually pale, "Your Highness, you . . . you have *visitors*."

"Visitors, Henri? What *kind* of visitors?"

I have to admit, I was taken completely off guard—not only because it had been so long since we'd had visitors of any kind at the palace (except ones who were protesting my mandates), but because our major domo, of all people, was freaking out and could no longer perform even the most basic aspect of his job description, which was to announce the name of any visitor to the palace.

"I . . . I don't know, Your Highness." Henri looked as if he were about to be sick. "I . . . remember them. They've been here before. But I—they—they've asked to see you, but they aren't wearing masks. I didn't want to risk being infected so I'm sorry to say that I . . . I . . . well, I forgot to ask." Henri was obviously mortified.

"Not wearing masks?" I was perplexed. "It's not Prince René, is it?"

"Oh, no, Your Highness. If it were, of course I would have alerted the Genovian Guard at once. No, this is . . . well, it's . . . it's . . ." He lowered his voice to a whisper. "It's *Americans*, Your Highness!"

This *was* a truly remarkable turn of events, considering the fact that Americans have been barred from entering the EU for some months now, unless of course they have dual citizenship. I could see now why Henri was so discomfited.

"Henri," I said, throwing back my shoulders. "Don't worry. I'll handle this."

Then, remembering that I have the blood of

warrior princesses running through my veins and should easily be able to handle some germ-infested Americans standing in my Great Hall, I stood up just as Elizabeth threw her gingerbread game piece down on the finish line and screamed, "Candyland! I won!"

"S***!" Frank shrieked, and threw his own game piece across the room.

Perhaps I'm not as brave a warrior princess as my ancestresses, since I yelled, "Play nicely, you two!" at my own children as I made my way toward the Grand Staircase. What is the point of yelling at toddlers? It's like yelling at people who won't wear masks. They refuse to understand, much less listen.

Honestly, though, what Americans would Lars have possibly allowed inside the palace gates? I assumed it had to be some random friends of Grandmère's—perhaps some that she and Derek had picked up at the yacht club (which has re-opened and is as busy as ever, though they've taken out some of the tables so the ones that remain are positioned six feet apart, outside only, and the employees are wearing masks. They require their patrons to wear masks, too, except for when they're eating and drinking, a rule with which Grandmère complies, but only because she ordered some limited-edition specialty designer five-hundred-dollar masks from Italy that she claims are "better for the delicate skin of the face" because they're made of pure silk. But they're completely useless since they've also got Swarovski crystals sewn onto them, leaving them riddled with holes).

But when I peeked my head over the balustrade of the Grand Staircase, the people I saw standing below weren't strangers.

"LANA?" I cried.

"Oh, hey, Mia!"

Lana Weinberger Rockefeller waved up at me, looking cool and chic in a pink and yellow sleeveless Pucci minidress. Her arms were tanned and muscular (she does Pilates daily in her home gym) and her blond hair flowed down her back in a flawless cascade.

Trust Lana to look so good during a global catastrophe.

I could hardly believe my eyes. "Wh-what are you doing here?"

"What do you mean?" She pulled off her Gucci sunglasses and squinted at me as I came down the stairs, Fat Louie fast on my heels—he follows me everywhere now. Since he's losing so much weight due to his hyperthyroidism, we give him people food in order to encourage him to eat, and he's always hoping to score a french fry or bite of Brie.

I was so stunned, I blurted out what I was thinking, instead of murmuring a polite *It's so good to see you*. "What are you doing here?"

"You told me I could come as soon as this thing was over," Lana said, beaming. "Well, here we are!"

"*We?*"

That's when I noticed Lana wasn't alone. Behind her was her equally tanned and good-looking husband, Jason, who had their four-year-old daughter, "Purple" Iris, by one hand and their new baby (now a chubby one-year-old) "Sir" Jason Rockefeller Junior in his arms.

"Hewwo, Pwincess!" Iris cried. Her hair was as blond and luxuriously wavy and long as her mother's, and she was lugging the cutest little Elsa from *Frozen* wheelie bag suitcase behind her. "Can Owivia come out and pway with me?"

"Um." I could not figure out what was happening. Not the part about Iris wanting to "play" with Olivia. Lana had visited before, and Olivia and her friends had babysat for Iris and even for Prince René's son, Morgan.

What I couldn't figure out was what Lana was doing, standing in the Great Hall of my palace, in the middle of a global pandemic.

"How exactly did you get here?" I finally managed to choke out.

"Oh, as soon as we saw on the news that you'd opened up your borders," Lana said, "Jason got right on the phone with his dad and wrangled the jet out of him. You can't *imagine* how horrible it is in East Hampton right now. The place is more crowded than SoHo on a Thursday night. You couldn't get a reservation to Nick & Toni's if your life depended on it, and that's even if you know the secret number! And the traffic? It's insane!

Why, it took an *hour* for Morell's to deliver our wine the other day. Oh, *merci beaucoup*."

Lana gratefully accepted a glass of champagne from the tray one of the footpersons hurried over to present to her and Jason, even though I certainly hadn't ordered any to be brought round. But I think Henri was so embarrassed by his gaffe, not formally announcing Lana's arrival to me, he'd had it sent out.

"So that's when we said, 'We just have to get out of here,'" Lana prattled on, "and ordered the jet. We went to Italy first, of course, because you know how much I love shopping in Milan. But can you believe it's closed? I mean, like, closed. *All* of it! So then I said, 'Honey, let's drop in on Mia, we missed Easter with her, and she said it would be fine as soon as the curb flattened or whatever.' So here we are!"

I just looked back through this diary, and that is so *not* what I said. This kind of thing is exactly why everyone should keep a diary, in fact, so they can look back on exactly what they *did* say, in order to prove people like Lana wrong.

Not that it makes any difference, of course, because a princess is always a gracious hostess. I can't exactly throw a mother of two and her husband out onto the street, even when they have multiple homes and a private jet. Not when there are people like René and his cronies outside the door—which, believe me, Lana commented on:

"Thank God Lars let us through the palace gates when he recognized us, or our limo driver from the airport might have had a coronary. What's René doing down there with all those people, waving those toy guns around, saying he doesn't want to wear masks?"

"Yeah," Jason said, guzzling his champagne. "I mean, what's the big deal? Just wear one, am I right?"

This was coming from someone who'd just gotten off a (private) plane from a foreign country with a significantly higher number of infections (and deaths) than mine, WHO WAS NOT WEARING A MASK.

"Uh," I said, wishing more than anything that Michael was around, because I was sure that he'd have been able to handle this socially awkward situation with ease, whereas I, despite being a princess, didn't have the slightest idea what to do. We're in an entirely new world now! There wasn't anything in any of the etiquette lessons Grandmère had given me about *this* kind of social situation.

But of course Michael was at his lab being a hero making his intranasal vaccines, and even Grandmère, who knows everything about manners, is suffering from some kind of psychotic break (possibly brought on by senility and/or too much sex with a much younger lover) and can no longer be depended on to do anything.

"Yeah," I said. "Well, René and I are having a slight disagreement about masking. Speaking of which—"

But before I could say another word, Iris sucked in her breath in an excited gasp, her large blue eyes springing wide, because Olivia had emerged from the French doors to the pool, wearing a swimsuit and sarong, looking strong and brown and sun-kissed and followed, as always, by her worshipful poodle Snowball and her even more worshipful boyfriend Prince Khalil (who, like Chad and Derek, has more or less been living with us since the start of the pandemic, although not in an official capacity, and he is of course much more welcome).

"*Owivia!*" Iris shrieked, and went careening toward my half sister like a three-foot-tall missile.

"Iris!" Ever gracious—unlike me—Olivia smiled, bent gracefully at the waist, and scooped up the little blond preschooler. "It's so good to see you!"

Iris shrieked in incoherent delight as Olivia spun her around. I should, as a concerned adult, have suggested that my little sister put down the probably germ-infested child, fresh off a jet from New York, and back away.

But I was at a loss for words. Who wouldn't be at finding a family of four in their home, unannounced, luggage in tow, even if that home happens to be a palace with more than enough guest bedrooms to accommodate them?

"How have you been?" Olivia asked Iris.

"I lost a toof!" Iris said, pointing at her mouth. "And there's bad men at your house with guns!"

"Oh, never mind them," Olivia said, cheerfully strolling over to look at "Sir" Jason Junior. "That's just our cousin Prince René and his friends. They're playing a game. Is this your new baby brother?"

"My bwuva!" Iris cried proudly, pointing at the baby in her father's arms. "He likes to swim, just like me. Can we go swimming now?"

"Yes, of course, darling. Niamh!" Lana called over her shoulder. "Help Iris find her swim things, will you?"

"Of course."

That's when I noticed it wasn't a family of four at all, but five, because there was a slender slip of a girl, so tiny that I hadn't noticed her at first (also possibly because she was loaded down with so many diaper bags, totes, and carry-ons, she looked more like a luggage rack than a human being).

But when Lana called, "Niamh!" she darted forward, and said, "I'm here," and I was able to see a face between all the Louis Vuitton. And a very pretty face it was.

"Oh, good," Lana said. "Mia, this is Niamh, our au pair. It's pronounced Neve, like Neve Campbell from *Party of Five*, remember that show? But it's spelled N-I-A-M-H, can you even believe it? Niamh is Irish. She's been a godsend during this awful time. I don't know what we'd have done without her. She's studying dance at NYU—"

"Dance therapy," Niamh corrected her employer, but very sweetly, and even managed to bob a polite curtsy in my direction, despite all the luggage she was carrying.

"Nice to meet you, Niamh," I said, and would have mentioned that I'd have known how to say Niamh and even more difficult to pronounce Irish names like Aoife and Siobhan without Lana's explanation since I've been to Ireland multiple times, but Lana didn't pause long enough in her breathless monologue to allow any interruptions.

I would have blamed this on the fact that we've all been in lockdown for so long that we've gotten a little rusty on our socialization skills, except that Lana has always been this way.

"Niamh got kicked out of the dorms when the university shut down due to the virus, which if you ask me was way overreacting," Lana raced on, "so we were more than happy to let her live with us so she didn't have to go home to Kerry—"

"Kilkerrin," Niamh said, kneeling down and opening one of the bags and wrestling Iris's bathing suit and water wings from it.

"—and the kids just adore her. And it's really been great for us, too, because we're helping a poor struggling college student from abroad in need."

"Uh-oh," Jason said, making a face and holding his son away from him. "I think someone just made another stinky boom-boom."

"I'll take care of it, sir." Niamh hurried over to lift Sir Jason from his father's arms.

"Well." I felt it was safe for me to say something, since Lana had apparently run out of steam—and champagne. The footperson was refilling her glass. "You're all welcome to stay here as long as you like." What else could I say? It wasn't like I could suggest they check into the Ritz instead. Lana was an old friend and besides, the Ritz was at 114 percent occupancy. They'd never get a bed, let alone a suite big enough to accommodate all of them. "I'll have some rooms made up for you in the east wing, where I'm sure you'll be very comfortable. In the meantime, why don't we head out to the pool with the children, and I'll ring for some lunch, if you're hungry?"

I didn't invite Lana and her family to a poolside lunch to be nice. I did it because I wanted to get them out of doors as quickly as possible, where they were less likely to infect my family and employees with whatever pathogens they might be carrying.

"Lunch would be amazing," an unsuspecting Lana cried. "I'm famished! And if Chef could make some more of that pear and gorgonzola salad like he did last time, that would be great. I've gained so much weight during this pandemic, I cannot even believe it!"

This coming from someone who, the last time

I'd made the mistake of going shopping with her, wore a size zero, and did not look as if she'd gained a pound, whereas I could not fit into a single one of my ball gowns. Not that I cared. There's a lot more to worry about right now than clothes.

"Where's my main man Mike?" Jason asked brightly. "Has he gotten the new version of *Call of Duty*? I bet he's upstairs playing it right now, isn't he? Hope he's ready to get thrashed!" Jason strode away from the pool, where I was trying to steer him, and toward the Grand Staircase, calling, "Mike! Hey, Mike!"

"Um," I said, as the major domo stared at me with eyes as wide as Genovian francs, "Michael is actually at work right now. But of course I'm happy to call him and let him know you're here."

"Work?" Both Lana and Jason laughed disbelievingly at this—not surprisingly, since neither of them had ever done a day of work in their lives.

Well, I shouldn't say that. Jason does do some day trading at a company that his family has owned for generations. And Lana had a brief stint as the singer/songwriter of the one-hit wonder "Put It in My Candyhole," which you can still occasionally hear sampled in underground German EDM (I only know this because Derek had played us some the other night).

"Yes," I said. "Michael and his team are working on a vaccine for the virus."

"*Here?*" Lana glanced around, alarmed. "He's got live virus here in the palace?"

"No, of course not. Michael has a lab downtown at his Pavlov Surgical offices. And the technology to make vaccines is so advanced these days that they don't need live samples of virus. They use DNA." I was only pretending that I understood how this DNA was then turned into what Michael kept referring to as RNA. "They're hoping to have their vaccine ready in a few weeks—"

"*Weeks?*" Lana looked stunned, but fortunately not enough to impede the progress we were making toward the pool. "But how can anyone create a vaccine that fast?"

"Yeah." Jason was already stripping off his shirt. "It must not be very safe."

"Actually," I said, "Michael says that this virus is very similar genetically to SARS and MERS—both coronaviruses that jumped from animals to people. We already had vaccine strategies in place for those, so it's not like we're starting from scratch creating a vaccine for COVID-19. So instead of waiting years or even months for a vaccine, it really only took weeks this time around. And since Michael's vaccine is intranasal, it's going to be needle-free and will deliver antigen directly to the site of infection. You do know that some of the very first vaccines were administered nasally by grinding up smallpox scabs and blowing them into the nostril, right?"

"Uh." Lana and Jason glanced at one another. "No."

"Oh, yes," I said. "In the late 1600s, Chinese emperor K'ang-hsi inoculated his own children against smallpox that way. In the 1700s, this practice caught on in Europe, though the method they used was variolation."

Both Lana and Jason looked as if they wished they hadn't asked. I could understand how they felt. I've been told by several people—including members of my own family—that they no longer wish to hear me quote whole passages from John M. Barry's book on the great influenza of 1918, or any book on any influenza, for that matter.

"Hello?" a woman's voice called out from the top of the Grand Staircase. "Did someone forget something up here?"

That's when Lilly appeared, with Frank and Elizabeth on either hip. They were each chewing on a Candyland pawn.

"Oh!" I couldn't believe I'd forgotten my own children in their playroom. "Hi, Lilly! Look who stopped by on their way from Italy."

Lilly stopped dead halfway down the stairs, her eyes bulging.

"Lilly!" Lana shrieked. "Hello! And Mia's babies! Oh my God! I can't believe how big you've gotten!"

It was unclear in the moment if Lana was referring to Lilly or my children.

"Lana," Lilly deadpanned. "It's you. With your

husband. And your kids. In Genovia. In the middle of a pandemic."

"S***," said Frank, and the game pawn tumbled from his lips.

That about summed up my feelings on the matter as well.

Quarantine Day One Billion

Poolside

All Lana wants to do is sit by the pool, drink wine, and gossip.

Wait, no—that's not all she wants to do.

She WANTS to go into town, eat in restaurants, shop, and dance in nightclubs.

But since Lilly and I won't do those things with her—me because I CAN'T since there's an uprising against me at the palace gates, staged by my own cousin, and also because I don't WANT to, due to the raging epidemic and the fact that most of the people visiting Genovia at the current time are refusing to wear masks, even though the Gendarmerie are doing a fairly good job of enforcing my mandate, but we don't want to cause an international incident, and the vast majority of the maskless are foreigners (WHERE are all these Americans coming from? I thought they weren't allowed to enter the EU?), and of course Lilly won't leave the palace gates at all in the company of Lana because it's Lana—she's stuck with sitting by the pool, drinking wine, and gossiping.

Not that I'm judging. AT ALL. Whatever people need to do in order to get through the day, hey, they should do it—so long as it doesn't infringe upon the rights of others.

And I have to say, some of Lana's gossip is pretty interesting.

"So," she said just now, while stretched out on one of the chaise lounges by the pool, watching Niamh play mermaid Barbies with our children.

I'm paying her double time to watch my kids in addition to Lana's. It's nice to give Olivia and her boyfriend a day off from childcare. I have no idea where they disappeared to. I just hope they're using birth control. I've given her a talk about it, which she listened to quite patiently until I got to the part about dental dams before finally saying, "Thanks so much, Mia, but your mother already told me all of this."

Of course. Of *course* my mother did.

Then Olivia added, "Prince Khalil and I are being very careful because when the pandemic is over, we intend to go to his native country, free it from its current oppressive regime through peaceful revolution, install a democratic government, then become epidemiologists so we can stop this kind of thing from happening again. We don't intend ever to have children because the earth is already overpopulated as it is."

"Oh," I said, blinking. "Okay."

Honestly, if you think about it, there is going to be an entire generation of kids with severe post-traumatic stress because of this whole thing (although Dr. Muhammad keeps saying children are very resilient. I certainly hope this is true, considering how many times Michael has playfully thrown Frank and Elizabeth into the air, only to cause them to hit their heads on the crystals of the palace's various four-hundred-year-old Venetian glass chandeliers).

Still, think about all the kids who lived through World War II and then went on to have very productive lives: sex therapist Dr. Ruth Westheimer, first female president of European Parliament Simone Veil, music promoter Bill Graham, even Grandmère, just to name a few.

Well, maybe I shouldn't include Grandmère.

"So," Lana said today, taking a sip of her pinot gris as she scrolled through her phone, "did you hear about Gupta?"

It took me a minute to figure out who she was talking about. Then I said, "You mean the principal of our high school?"

Lana nodded so hard that the floppy brim of her sun hat bounced up and down.

"Yes. Only she's not principal anymore. She's been promoted to superintendent of schools."

"What?" I nearly choked on my own wine. Because of course I was drinking, too, even though it was only one in the afternoon. I wasn't going to let Lana drink alone. Well, alone with Lilly. And

Grandmère. And Jason and Chad and Derek, who were taking a break from playing *Call of Duty* in the pool house.

"Of course!" Lana cried. "You don't think the New York City school system was going to let talent like that go to waste, do you?"

"No," I said. "It makes sense. But how do you even know this?"

"Because, silly, I put Iris and Sir Jason on the waitlist for Albert Einstein."

"But it's going to be years before they're ready for high school!"

"Yes, but getting kids into the good schools has gotten so competitive these days. You have to be aggressive. I want my kids to have the best education the city has to offer. Jason thinks we should send them to Dalton—"

"I'm not saying there's anything wrong with Albert Einstein—" Jason tried to chime in, but his wife cut him off.

"—but getting your kids into the right college is so important, and I don't want my kids to look like all the others applying from Manhattan. I want them to *stand out*, not be some cookie-cutter version of all the others. That's why I think *diversity* is just as important to a child's education as anything else," Lana said. "Niamh, say something to Iris in Gaelic."

Niamh, in the pool, said something incomprehensible to Purple Iris, who babbled cheerfully back at her.

"See?" Lana beamed at me. "I want my children to be fluent in multiple languages."

"Wow," Lilly said, from her own chaise lounge. "People speak so much Gaelic these days, especially in business settings."

"I know," Lana said proudly, Lilly's sarcasm flying, as usual, straight over her head. "Speaking of Albert Einstein High, did you hear about poor Perrin and Ling Su?"

"Mia's lesbian couple friends?" Grandmère screeched.

I wanted to die. *"Grandmère."*

"Well, they are." Grandmère turned to Chad and Derek. "My granddaughter is friends with several lesbians."

"Cool," Derek said.

"So," Lana went on, oblivious as always to the interruption, "they're having a baby. Well, Ling Su is. I guess Perrin will be the dad. Well, obviously the sperm donor is the biological dad. But Perrin will be the, er, actual dad."

"Yes, Lana," I said. Why did everyone think I wasn't in touch with any of my former classmates, many of whom were close friends? "I actually know all this. Perrin and Ling Su operate the teen community center I opened in Manhattan in my stepfather Frank's name. Remember? You were there for the opening ceremony. You made a very generous donation."

"Oh," Lana said. "Right. I forgot."

"That community center is nice," Jason said,

taking a big slurp of the piña colada he'd ordered. "It has a really sweet rock-climbing wall."

"Okay," Lana said, still scrolling through her phone, "but did you hear about Shameeka?"

Grandmère announced loudly enough to be heard by everyone within hearing distance, including the gardener who was pruning the nearby rose-bushes, "Oh, yes, Shameeka! My granddaughter also has an *African American friend.*"

I dropped my head into my hands. "*Grandmère.*"

"What?" Grandmère looked perplexed. "You do."

"You have an African American *granddaughter,*" I reminded her. "Olivia. Remember?"

"Of course," Grandmère said. "But family can't choose us. Our friends can. And Shameeka *chooses* to be friends with you, Amelia. Even though she was very popular in high school, unlike you. But many of us go through an awkward stage during adolescence. Except for Shameeka, of course, she was always attractive. Now she does marketing work for the fashion designer Vera Wang."

I stared up at the sky and contemplated death.

"Yes," Lana said, waving her phone at me, on which there was now an Instagram post showing Shameeka and a very tall man looking amazing on the balcony of a hotel in South Beach. "*And* she's dating a New York Knick."

"She has my deepest sympathies," Jason quipped.

He was on his third cocktail, keeping brisk pace with Grandmère.

"Oh, and of course you know about Kenny," Lana went on, as if no one else around her were talking, her custom where everyone, including her husband, is concerned.

"No," I said. Okay, maybe I wasn't in touch with *all* of my former classmates. "What about Kenny?"

"Mia, how can you not know about Kenny? Are you not on Insta or anything?"

"No, Mia's not on social media," Lilly said, sounding animated. This was one of her favorite subjects. "She had her assistant take away all her passwords so she would stop Googling herself and seeing the negative comparisons people were making of her to all the other princesses in the world."

"Aw." Lana gave my bare knee a sympathetic pat. "I understand. You have to take care of your mental health. Anyway, your ex-boyfriend, Kenny, finally moved out of his tepee and got a job as a truck driver, which is good because we really need truck drivers right now to deliver our toilet paper and other badly needed supplies, like lip filler. See?"

Lana showed Lilly and me a photo on her phone of someone who looked vaguely like a much older, weathered version of Kenny Showalter, leaning casually against the cab of an enormous big rig.

The rig wasn't the only thing that was big. The

biceps of the guy in the profile pic were humongous, as was the bulge at the front of the faded jeans he wore.

Lilly nearly spat out the sip of wine she'd taken. "There is *no way* that's Kenny."

"It is," Lana insisted. "Only now he calls himself Ken. Ken Showalter."

Lilly leaned back against her chaise, shaking her head. "Wow. And to think, Mia, he could have been yours, only you let him get away."

I rolled my eyes. "He was your ex more recently than he was mine, Lilly, so *you* let him get away."

Lilly pulled her sun hat down over her eyes, all animation shut down. "I'm not interested in men," she said. "Anymore."

This was news to me, considering how many times I'd seen her sneaking off into Lars's apartment in the Genovian guard's quarters. But who knew? Maybe she was sneaking into Serena's apartment.

"Are you a lesbian, too, now, Lilly?" Grandmère asked brightly. To the rest of us she remarked, conversationally, "I experimented with lesbianism in college, you know. Well, who didn't? It's what young people do. I understand that makes me bisexual."

I spat out the sip of wine I'd taken. *"Grandmère!"*

"What?" Grandmère looked around innocently. "You yourself said that you want the twins to feel free to experiment with their sexuality so they won't experience—what is it again? Oh, yes—gender dysphoria when they're older, Amelia. I assume that's why you're allowing little Frank to play with that mermaid doll over there."

"They can play with whatever they want," I exclaimed. "As long as they don't light anything on fire. I just don't want—"

"Bisexual!" Frank yelled merrily from the pool.

"—that to happen." I shot my grandmother a now-you've-done-it look. Were we to be treated to cries of bisexual from the twins all day long going forward?

Not that I mind. I am all about inclusivity and consider myself an ally. I make sure the rainbow flag is flown all month at the palace and all Genovian embassies during Pride.

But I have heard—and witnessed—way more than I cared to lately about my grandmother's sexuality.

"Oh, if you're not online much, Mia, then you probably don't know the really big news—the thing everyone is talking about." Lana waved her phone around.

"I'm sure I don't." What could be bigger than the news the Dowager Princess of Genovia had just delivered?

"I'm bisexual, too," I overheard Niamh say shyly from the pool, where she was steering Elizabeth, Frank, Iris, and Sir Jason around on an enormous inflatable raft shaped like a unicorn.

I think I was the only person who noticed both

Chad and Derek glance her way. "Are you, now?" Derek's eyebrows were raised.

"How *delightful*!" Grandmère declared, clapping her hands. "Perhaps we should have Chef make a cake for dessert tonight to celebrate?"

"That sounds *great*, Grandmère," called Rocky from the diving board where he was preparing to execute a pike. "Can it have a molten lava center?"

"I don't see why not."

OH. MY. GOD.

Lana, looking annoyed that no one was paying attention to her, sat up and announced: "TINA HAKIM BABA AND BORIS PELKOWSKI BROKE UP!"

Quarantine Day

One Billion, continued

Royal Bedroom

I'm the worst friend in the entire world.

If I were a good friend, I'd have spent less time worrying about what was happening within my own palace gates and more time looking outside them (and I don't mean right outside them, at my cousin and his friends).

If I had once—just once—looked at a television station that wasn't Genovian 24/7 news, or clicked on a link that wasn't about the worrying rise in infections here, I'd have seen that international pop sensation Boris P (as he is now known) had split with his longtime girlfriend and fiancée, New York City surgeon (and one of my best friends) Tina Hakim Baba.

What's worse is that she never told me!

But it's not as if I'd asked. I had had to hear it from Lana Weinberger Rockefeller, of all people.

And true, Tina and Boris haven't had the smoothest of relationships. They break up and get together more often than my grandmother and, well, her many, many boyfriends (and apparently girlfriends).

But still. I should have been paying closer attention.

I FaceTimed Tina as soon as I heard (actually, as soon as I could get the children out of the pool, fed, and down for their afternoon naps).

Anyway, Tina picked up my call, but that didn't mean she wasn't at work. She was only on a break, her plastic face shield shoved up above her red-rimmed eyes, her KN95 mask pushed down beneath her chin, her lips chapped but determined.

"Oh, Tina," I said. "I just heard. Why didn't you tell me?"

"I—I just couldn't," she said, with a brave attempt at a smile. "You never liked Boris anyway, remember?"

"Of course I did," I lied. "I learned to like Boris. And *you* liked him. And that's what's important. You *loved* him! And I love you, so you know I always want to be here for you."

"Well," she said, shrugging her too-slim shoulders beneath her protective paper gown. Tina's always been on the well-nourished side, but too many hours at a too-demanding job were causing the pounds to melt off her, and not in a healthy way. "It doesn't matter now. He made the decision to walk, and that's fine with me."

"But *why*?" I couldn't imagine a world where someone like Boris Pelkowski would walk away from someone like Tina Hakim Baba. Tina leaving Boris, yes, of course. Boris is and always has been ridiculous. But Tina? Tina is one of the most fantastic people I've ever met. "How could he possibly break up with you? You're the best thing that's ever happened to him—to anyone."

Tina shrugged again. Her normally sparkling brown eyes looked dull and listless. For that alone, I could have killed Boris.

"I couldn't give him what he wants. And that's a partner who's always there for him."

"What are you talking about?" I cried. *"Of course* you're always there for him. Who helped him overcome the panic attack he got the first time he was supposed to perform live at Wembley Stadium? That was you. You're the best girlfriend in the world!"

Tina: "No, he means *literally* always be there for him. He wants me to give up my job and move with him into the thirty-million-dollar beach house he just bought in Malibu. I know to most girls that would sound amazing. But I love my job. I don't want to leave it. I feel like I'm really making a difference in people's lives, especially now."

Lilly (because she was sitting nearby, wanting to be in on the call): "Well, of course you are! Mia, tell her she's making a huge difference."

Me: "Lilly says to tell you that of course you're making a huge difference."

Tina smiled a little and wiped away the tears that had begun to drop down her beautifully rounded cheeks.

Tina: "Thanks. I know I am. It just hurts that he thinks I'm going to give up so many years of school to go and simply—I don't know. *Live.* He says that with this pandemic, we don't know how much time we've got left, so we should try to enjoy it to the fullest, at his new house, complete with an infinity pool and built-in firepit, right on the beach, where you can see gray whales in the distance."

Mia: "Well, I have to admit that does sound kind of nice—the whales . . ."

Lilly: "What? No, it doesn't! It sounds completely ridiculous! He's gaslighting you. Is he giving up *his* career?"

Tina (shaking her head): "No. He's livestreaming acoustic concerts for his fans. He charges sixty dollars a ticket through Crowdcast."

Lilly: "Then *screw him*! Let him go live

in his beach house alone, or with some
ditzy groupie who doesn't have a career.
A career *saving people's lives*, like you do,
Tina."

Tina: "That's what I said to him. Never in
a million years did I think he'd actually do
it. But he did."

Me: "He's found someone else?"

Tina: "Well, no, not that I know of. Not
yet. But I'm sure he will. He's got two
hundred million followers to choose from."

Me: "Oh, Tina. I'm so sorry. But you know,
maybe you two just need a little break.
You've probably noticed that a lot of
normally levelheaded people are freaking
out right now."

Lilly: "Yeah! Especially men. Because
they're weak!"

I gave her a dirty look.

Me: "Not all men are weak. Some of them,
like my husband, are quite strong. But it's
true that some men—and women, too—
don't seem emotionally capable of coping
with the reality of a crisis like COVID. Like

my cousin René, who thinks the appropriate
way to cope with it is to hold an anti-mask
protest outside my palace gates right now.
And you wouldn't believe who hopped on
a jet and showed up at my front door the
other day—"

Lilly: "You think *Lana* is normally
levelheaded?"

Me: "Well, her emotional intelligence has
grown over the years."

Lilly (shrugging): "I guess, if you compare
her to your relatives, and a mouth-breather
like Bor—"

Holding my phone away from my face, I made a
violent slashing motion beneath my chin, whisper-
ing "Stop" to Lilly. "What if they get back together?
You know they're going to. They always do."

Lilly rolled her eyes. "I don't think so," she
said, not bothering to whisper. "Not this time.
They're obviously completely incompatible. Look
how they react in a crisis. Tina wants to save lives,
and Boris wants to bury his head in the sand—
literally, on a beach in Malibu—and pretend like
nothing bad is happening."

"It's true," Tina said. When I righted my phone
and looked at her, it was clear she'd overheard
everything Lilly had said. "We are incompatible.

And yes, you're right to blame COVID. It's really helped to show people's true colors. During an emergency, some people run to help, some people run away, and some people just stand there. And Boris has turned out to be someone who runs. It's so sad to me that he isn't stronger than he is, because I always thought he and I were going to have a fairy-tale ending, like you and Michael, Mia. But it turns out that it's only in romance novels that everyone gets a happily-ever-after."

My heart ached to hear her say this—ached with sadness for her, because Tina has always been the staunchest supporter of romance that I've ever known, and ached in anger toward Boris for letting her down. I searched frantically inside for the right thing to say to her . . . anything to drive the listless despair from her big brown eyes.

"Come on, Tina," I said. "I know things are bad right now, but you know as well as I do that you and Boris will work things out, and have the romantic wedding you always dreamed of—"

She cut me off.

"No, Mia. I don't think we will. I thought Boris was my soul mate. And maybe he was—for a while. Maybe there are people who are right for you at the right time. But if things get tough and that person runs, you have to acknowledge that it's time to move on. And that's what I'm doing. Anyway, enough about me. How are you two doing? Tell me more about Lana. Did she really just show up without being invited? That's so Lana."

Lilly threw a pillow at me and whispered, "Tell her that your grandmother is bisexual. That will cheer her up."

I made another shut-up motion with my hand to try to get Lilly to stop, but she just kept going.

"Tina," Lilly yelled, apparently because it was clear I wasn't going to say anything. "Mia's grandmother announced at the pool today that she's bisexual!"

Tina looked perplexed. "What?"

"It's true," I said, while sending Lilly a dirty look. "Although there's nothing funny about it. Her sexuality is her business."

"Of course," Tina said. "There's obviously nothing wrong with it."

"Right. I will support my grandmother whatever she chooses." (Although to be honest I'd much prefer she marry Niamh than Derek if she has to marry any impoverished college student.)

"Of course you will," Tina said. "When's the wedding?"

"Hopefully never," I said. "She wants to have a big blowout ceremony and reception, which I think is a really bad idea right now. Maybe after we have a vaccine."

"A lot of people are delaying their weddings until then," Tina said in a voice so wistful, I could tell that she'd been planning the same thing—

until stupid Boris pulled his whole "give up your job and move with me into my beach house" stunt.

I realized I needed to change the subject or Tina was going to start crying again.

"I guess it's great Grandmère has found love late in life," I said in a voice that sounded fake, even to myself. "I just can't help wishing I had a *normal* grandmother who baked me cookies and gave me wise advice, like grandmothers in Hallmark Channel movies, and didn't overshare about her sex life with me."

"Oh, yes." Tina nodded. "That would be nice." My ruse had worked. She was completely distracted. "You know, Mia, speaking of oversharing, something we're seeing a lot of lately in our older patients since COVID is mild neurocognitive impairment—nothing significant enough to interfere with their daily activities, but enough to impair their memory and social skills."

"Oh," I said. "Trust me, my grandmother doesn't have COVID. We test her regularly because she's always lunching at the yacht club, which is just a hotbed of infection, and she's always negative."

Tina: "I'm not talking about that. I'm talking about elderly patients whose normal cognitive function has become mildly impaired due to the social isolation brought on by this pandemic."

Lilly (snorting): "The last thing Clarisse has been during this pandemic is socially isolated."

Tina: "I'm glad to hear that. But for many of the elderly, their normal routines and social circles have been so vastly disrupted, they've become . . . well, C and C is what we call it at the hospital where I work."

Me: "C and C?"

Tina: "Cranky and crazy. I'm sorry. I know the word *crazy* is stigmatizing, and of course I would never use it in front of a patient. Mental illness is a serious issue, and affects all of us. But for so many of the elderly patients we're seeing right now, cranky and crazy is the only way to sum up what they're going through. It could explain . . . well, why your grandmother is insisting on having a large wedding to a nineteen-year-old college student."

Lilly: "But with Clarisse, how could you even tell? Cranky and crazy is her normal disposition."

Me: "Oh, come on. My grandmother has never been *this* bad."

But even as I came to my grandmother's defense, I was thinking to myself that "cranky and crazy" was a good way to describe a lot of her behavior lately. Maybe there was something to Tina's theory.

And maybe it didn't extend only to the elderly, but to younger people as well. It would explain René's behavior, and Boris's as well. Perhaps the whole world's gone C and C.

Even me.

NOTE TO SELF: Look up Grandmère's symptoms later on WebMD. Although if you ask me, her neurocognition has been impaired for the entirety of the time I've known her.

Quarantine Day Who Cares?
Royal Bedroom

*J*ust told Michael that he has to call Boris and tell him that he needs to step up and act right where Tina is concerned.

"Since when is it *my* job to supervise Boris Pelkowski?" Michael wanted to know.

"Since you were bar mitzvahed at age thirteen," I said, "and became a man."

"What?" Michael was playing horsey with Frank and Elizabeth, bouncing each of them on his knees with such enthusiasm that I suspected they'd eventually spit up their supper.

But if he stopped, they'd cry for him to continue. Such is the way with two-year-olds.

"It's the *real Call of Duty*," I explained. "The duty of all men to make sure other men aren't acting like total jerks, like Boris is currently doing to poor Tina."

"What makes you think Boris would even listen to me?" Michael asked.

"Because he looks up to you. You're like the cool older brother he never had."

Michael grinned. "You think I'm cool? I thought

I was a nerd who talks too much about RNA and needs to shave off his beard and sideburns."

I leaned over to stroke his face. "Well, maybe you only need to trim them a little."

"Mommy horsey ride, too!" the twins screamed, grabbing fistfuls of my cardigan.

"No." I tried to extricate myself before I tumbled down onto Michael's lap. "No horsey ride for Mommy right now."

Michael's grin turned lustful as he snaked an arm around my waist. "Mommy can go for a horsey ride on Daddy anytime she wants."

Suddenly we were all in a pile on the sofa, the twins shrieking delightedly, and Michael kissing me.

I have to admit, sometimes being in lockdown—even with my grandmother and Lana Weinberger Rockefeller—isn't the worst thing in the world.

Quarantine Day

???

Royal Bedroom

$\mathcal{D}$ad was just here. Since he *never* stops by my bedroom (because it used to be his room, but now it's my room that I share with a BOY, even though that boy is a full-grown man to whom I am married, and who my dad actually likes, even if Michael doesn't play golf or follow Formula 1 racing), I knew something was wrong.

Me: "What do you want?"

Dad: "Can't a father just want to spend time with his daughter?"

Me: "Not if that father is you."

Dad: "You've cut me to the quick. Really, Mia? A wine fridge next to the bed? What happened to that nightstand that used to be there? That belonged to Marie Antoinette. It had a built-in commode."

Me: "Get to the point, Dad. I have a country to run."

Dad: "All right. You've got to do something about your grandmother."

Me: "My *grandmother*? She's *your* mother. Why don't *you* do something about her?"

Dad: "You know she's never listened to me. But you're the one in charge now. You can actually do something to put a stop to this lunatic wedding she's planning to that . . . that . . . whatever he is."

Me: "You told me not to worry about it! I went to you when they first got engaged and you said that the whole thing was only a distraction, and that she'd never go through with it!"

Dad: "Well, that's what I thought, *then*. Obviously I was wrong. What kind of man agrees to marry a woman *four times* his age?"

Me: "That's what I tried to tell you! You're only just now coming to realize that Derek is only interested in Grandmère's money?"

Dad: "Well, it certainly isn't her looks he's attracted to."

Me: "Dad, that's ageist. Grandmère is quite fit for someone who was around during D-Day."

Dad: "If you say so. You've still got to stop this ridiculous charade. Did you hear she's going around telling people she's bisexual now? She's even got your children saying it!"

Me: "Have you ever thought of seeing a therapist to discuss why it is that you're so threatened by your mother's sexual orientation?"

Dad: "Dammit, Mia! I *do* see a therapist. Er, well, I see your mother's therapist, *with* your mother, when she forces me to go. So I know that I need to be less rigid and more open about my feelings. I also know that you often use humor as a defense mechanism and to deflect conflict."

Whoa. I was not in any way prepared for this particular truth bomb.

Me: "Dad. Way to go! That is such a huge step forward for you!"

Dad: "Mia, please. My mother? You'll talk to her?"

Me: "I've tried. I'll try again. As much as anyone can talk to Grandmère. You know that my friend Tina was saying that some of her older patients are suffering from mild cognitive impairment brought on by the isolation of the pandemic."

Dad: "That is hardly your grandmother. She's the least isolated person I know. In fact, I wish she'd consider isolating herself more."

Me: "That's what I said. But I looked it up, and she does have many of the symptoms and risk factors—she smokes, drinks, doesn't get very much exercise—except when she's dancing on yachts—and is so old, the birth certificates they issued during the time she was born must have been written on papyrus, because hers has crumbled to dust and disappeared."

Dad: "I think we should ask Derek how much exercise she's getting."

Me: "Ew, Dad!"

Dad: "You're right. That was beneath me."

Me: "You really are fixated on your mother's sex life. I would definitely bring that up at your next therapy appointment."

Dad: "Thank you, Mia. That is so helpful. By which I mean, not at all helpful. So how, exactly, are we supposed to find out if my mother really is suffering from this cognitive impairment, or whatever it is?"

Me: "Well, get her to a doctor, I suppose."

Dad: "How is that supposed to happen? Unless we tell her it's a plastic surgeon, your grandmother would sooner drop dead than visit a doctor."

Me: "I don't know. I was hoping you had an idea."

Dad: "You speak daily with Dr. Khan about the virus numbers. Can't you mention it to her?"

Me: "Is that even ethical?"

Dad: "Is it ethical of that college boy to be taking advantage of an elderly woman in her current mental state?"

Me: "I'm not entirely sure who is taking advantage of who in that situation."

Dad: "Just ask Dr. Khan about it next time you speak with her, Mia!"

Me: "God, fine. I will!"

Dad: "Good. Thank you."

Dad looked around the room one more time. "I'm starting to wonder if we aren't all suffering from some sort of cognitive impairment because of this damned pandemic," he said, his gaze on the wine fridge. Then he walked out of my room.

I wonder if Mom's therapist gives discounts on family sessions.

Quarantine Day Who Knows?

Palace Rose Garden

I am . . . I don't even know. How is it that every single day lately just seems to get worse and worse?

I was trying to have a serious discussion with Dr. Khan about my grandmother potentially having dementia when I got interrupted.

And interrupted in the worst possible way.

"I could of course give her a mental status exam," Dr. Khan was saying. She was sounding somewhat bewildered since we'd just been in the middle of our weekly COVID update via Zoom, this time about resuming masked in-school learning (remote learning was going horribly, as illustrated by the fact that Rocky now has the highest score on *Call of Duty* of anyone in my household, including Chad, Derek, Khalil, Michael, Jason, Serena, and Lars, but is getting straight Fs in school). "But it ought properly to be done by a neurologist. Might I ask, does your grandmother know what day it is?"

I scoffed. "No one knows what day it is."

"Well, yes," Dr. Khan agreed. "But is your

grandmother aware of her surroundings in general?"

"Who can say?" I glanced out the window. I was Zooming from my office and could see Grandmère sitting by the pool, jabbering away to Lana, while the twins splashed around on their unicorn floatie with Niamh and Derek and Lana's kids. "Yesterday a gigantic box arrived. It contained five thousand cocktail napkins, monogrammed with a crown and the initials *C & D*. Does that sound like someone who is aware of her surroundings?"

"It's very difficult to say." Dr. Khan looked thoughtful. "Could you have her draw the face of a clock for me, and ask her to put the exact time on it?"

I knew what she was getting at. As a consummate hypochondriac, I'd both seen the movie *and* read the book *Brain on Fire*, and knew that if a patient drew the numbers of a clock all crowded together on one side, it could indicate anti-NMDA receptor encephalitis.

But how was I supposed to get the Dowager Princess of Genovia to draw anything at all?

"Grandmère is going to ask why I want her to draw a clock," I said. "And then she's going to ask me why I don't get one of the palace staff to tell me what time it is if I need to know so badly. I can hardly slip a request like that in between the seating chart she's struggling with for the wedding reception. She's still trying to decide where to put

Meghan and Harry. She can't exactly not invite the queen, but what about the rest of the Windsors? Especially Prince Andrew. Everything is so awkward right now."

"Oh, I know," the prime minister said. Because of course the mental health of Genovia's oldest living royal was her business, so I wasn't going to leave her out of the conversation. "Tell her it's for a contest! Your grandmother is quite competitive, Princess. She once challenged me to a schnapps-drinking contest. Tell her the clock-drawing thing is for a prize."

This was no help whatsoever.

But fortunately—or so I thought, then—we were interrupted by the major domo, who came in wearing a KN95 mask, a plastic face shield, and an expression that was even paler and deathlier serious than usual.

"I'm so sorry to interrupt, Your Highness," he said.

Since my weekly meetings with Dr. Khan, the prime minister, and Dr. Muhammad are sacrosanct and never to be disturbed, I knew it had to be something extremely important. Except that I could see that Grandmère had not stirred from her place by the pool, and the twins were fine, if the fact that they were gleefully screaming swear words at their great-grandmother's dog could be considered fine.

"What is it, Henri?" I asked, thinking that René and his cronies must finally have breached the palace walls and be on their way up to arrest—or perhaps sneeze on—me.

But I couldn't hear any shouting, and I knew if anyone had slipped past the guard, the security system would have sounded, and I'd already have been swept into my safe room (location redacted for security reasons).

"His Highness Prince Michael asked me to let you know that Mister Boris P is here." It looked as if it pained Henri greatly to have to utter the words *Boris P.*

I must have stared at the major domo for a full thirty seconds before his words registered. "Boris? Boris is *here*?"

"Yes, Your Highness." Henri bowed, so stiffly that his powdered wig remained perfectly in place. "Prince Michael telephoned from his laboratory with his regrets that he could not greet Mister, uh, P himself, as he is on the cusp of publicly launching his vaccine. But he presumed you'd wish to see Mister P, as from what I understand he has a message to share with you that is of a somewhat, er, urgent nature? Shall I bring tea? Or champagne?" Glancing at my face, he said, "Or perhaps something stronger?"

I glanced back at my computer screen and said, "Ladies, I'm afraid we'll have to continue this discussion at another time."

"Of course," said Dr. Muhammad. "But did he just say Boris P, as in Boris P the worldwide rock sensa—"

"Take me to him," I said to the major domo, reaching to log off.

"Please tell Boris I'm his biggest fan!" I heard Dr. Muhammad cry, just as I was closing my laptop. "I have all his—"

CLICK.

This is all my fault, I thought to myself as I followed the major domo downstairs. I'd sent a man to do a job—talk Boris into not being such an idiot—that ought to have been done by a woman. Although Michael is exemplary at most things—lovemaking, using a computer, being a dad, protecting his loved ones against the threat of a deadly virus by inventing an intranasal vaccine for it—he isn't good at *everything*. No one can be.

And one thing Michael isn't good at is talking sense into worldwide rock sensations. I should never have asked him to do it.

So *of course* Boris had ended up here. And now I have to deal with him. What else had I expected to happen?

I'll tell you what I *hadn't* expected to happen: what came next.

Henri, apparently having learned from the Lana incident, had parked Boris in the Rose Garden, where I could visit with him out of doors and not contract whatever viral load he might be carrying with him. I found him sitting on one of the centuries-old marble benches with his elbows on his knees and his head in his hands, much like Rodin's *The Thinker*, only fortunately (for me) not naked.

"Boris?" I said, because he looked so dejected—and his hair had grown out so much since I'd last seen him, it was now flowing in wild curls down either side of his face—I actually didn't recognize him at first.

Then his head popped up and I saw that those eyes, streaming with tears, could only belong to one person: the boy we'd locked in the closet so many times in high school because he wouldn't stop playing such gloomy concertos—Bartók! Why did it always have to be Bartók?—on his violin.

"Oh, Mia," he cried, attempting to throw himself dramatically into my arms.

"Uh, no, no," I said, quickly sidestepping his embrace. "Social distancing, please. You've just been on a plane."

"Oh." Boris looked even more dejected, if such a thing were possible. "But it was my own plane. And they just gave me a rapid test at the airport. I'm negative."

"Never mind that now." I sat down on a marble bench across from his. "What are you doing here?"

"Oh, I had to come." Boris sighed dramatically and slumped back down on his own bench, looking out of place—or maybe completely in place—in his leather jeans, puffy-sleeved white shirt, scruffy beard, and black Converse high-tops. "I didn't know where else to turn. After Michael said I was being a dick—"

"I'm sorry." My eyebrows were raised to their limits. "Michael called you a what?"

"No. That's right. He didn't say I was a dick. He said I was *acting* like a dick. To Tina."

"Oh." Well, it wasn't untrue. Still, Michael had received a great deal of etiquette training as my prince consort—not as much as I had, as the actual regent, but a lot—and I'm fairly certain some of it had entailed instruction in not calling people, or telling them that they were acting like, dicks. I suppose it was good that in this case, however, Michael had stayed true to his instincts.

"I've tried to apologize to her a million times, but she won't return my messages. Maybe she's blocked me. I don't know. Mia, you're her best friend. She'll listen to you. You've got to help me. Please!"

"Well," I said. "You *were* very rude to her, Boris."

"I know!" Boris leaped to his feet, clutching his shaggy head. "I've made the worst mistake of my life. I don't know what I was thinking. I just thought—she's going to be my wife! I want to be supportive of her! I want her to have everything, you know? The best life she can have. Not be around all that death and misery. So when my real estate agent showed me the house, I bought it. I thought it was the most beautiful place I'd ever seen. Like this one."

He gestured across the roses, toward the sparkling sea below us, dotted with megayachts. "I wanted to give it to her. If someone bought *you* a thirty-million-dollar beach house in Malibu, wouldn't *you* quit your crappy hospital job to go and live in it?"

"Well," I said slowly. "I don't know. But, Boris, it doesn't matter what *I* would do. Tina's the one who's always dreamed of being a doctor. You're not being supportive of her by asking her to give up her dream. What would you say if she asked you to give up your dream of being a musician?"

"I'd do it," Boris said, raking his fingers through his hair, and causing his curls to stand even more riotously on end. "Especially if by being a musician I was putting my life at risk every single day."

I couldn't help it: I laughed at him. "No, you wouldn't. You couldn't stop playing music any more than you could stop breathing."

I wanted to say, "breathing out of your mouth instead of your nose," but he's honestly gotten better at that since having his Bionator removed.

"I *would*," he insisted. "I would if Tina asked me to! I'd do anything she asked me to, because I love Tina more than music. I love Tina more than I love my own life!"

He shouted this dramatically enough that some of the tourists and even some of the protesters down at the palace gates turned to look, though fortunately I was shielded by the roses and no one could see that I was sitting there with love-addled Boris P.

"Well," I said, "if that's true, then you should love Tina enough to support her dreams. And Tina's dream is to be a doctor, not a rich housewife of Malibu. One of the most important parts of being in a relationship is supporting your partner's dreams, as long as they aren't hurting anyone—and Tina's dream is to save people, not hurt them. If you really love Tina as much as you say you do, try supporting her instead of attempting to change her into someone she's not."

Boris stopped his wild pacing and hair-raking to stare at me in shock. "My God," he breathed. "Is that what I've been doing?"

"Yes," I said. "If you want some cute little wife who's going to do nothing but shop and do her nails and make smoothies for you or whatever, I'm sure you could find one. But that's not going to be Tina."

"I don't want that," Boris said. All the blood had drained out of his face, causing his stubby whiskers to stand out in even starker contrast to his pale skin. "I don't want that at all! I just want Tina. But I want her to be safe. And happy."

"Well, the only way Tina is going to be happy is if she's out there risking her own life by saving others. That's just how she is." I rose, hoping we were done. "Now, I'm sure you'd like to phone her and apologize for how selfish you've been. So I'll just leave you alone so you can do—"

"Your Highness." Unfortunately, one of the footpersons appeared, bearing an ice bucket containing an open bottle of champagne on ice and two glasses. "Where would you like me to put this?"

"Oh, *thank you.*" Boris pounced on the champagne. "I really need this."

I sank back down onto my bench. I was never getting out of there.

Were social interactions always this difficult, or was it simply that all my friends and relatives have become more annoying as time—or this pandemic—has gone on?

"I should have come to you about this much sooner," Boris said, guzzling down champagne like it was water. He didn't even offer me any. Not that I wanted some. It was, after all, only eleven o'clock in the morning, and I've really been trying not to start drinking alcohol before noon, like a civilized person. "Do you think if I tell her we'll only use the place in Malibu for holidays and vacations, Tina would take me back?"

"I really couldn't say." I was going to have to speak to the staff about bringing out little cookies or cheese sticks or something with the champagne when we have lovesick guests drop by so they have something to fill their stomachs and don't get so drunk right away.

"I wish Tina and I were more like you and Michael," Boris mourned. "You two get along so well. I practically wanted to throw up when Michael was telling me all about your perfect life here, with him working all day in his lab and you here in the castle, raising your perfect twins and looking so beautiful and running the country so successfully."

"Well," I said, trying not to sound smug. Because of course he was right. I am beautiful and am running the country more or less successfully, and the twins *are* perfect. "I suppose it might seem a bit idyllic to an outsider. But we do have our challenges." I wasn't going to mention Grandmère, or Derek, or Lana, or the fact that just that morning the twins had tried to flush Michael's watch down the bidet.

"Oh, I know." Boris tossed back more champagne. "Michael told me all about Fat Louie."

Excuse me? Michael complained to Boris about Fat Louie?

Well, I suppose sharing a bed with an ancient cat who frequently vomits up pool water (if I'm perfectly honest, sometimes on the sheets, while we're under them) can be challenging.

"And of course he told me about that idiot cousin of yours," Boris went on. "Trying to arrest you, or whatever. Not to mention your sugar momma grandma. But still. The two of you seem so chill together. You don't even mind about Judith." Boris shook his head at me in admiring disbelief. "I always knew you'd matured a lot since high school. Remember when you didn't even want to be a princess? But not even caring that Michael is collaborating with his ex-girlfriend on this vaccine? That is just *beyond* chill. I wish I could be like that. I wish *Tina* could be like that. She is not at *all* chill about my fans, and I'm not chill about the doctors she works with. Some of those guys are pretty good-looking. Not as good-looking as the ones on *Grey's Anatomy*, but—"

"I'm sorry." I could tell that the smile I'd plastered onto my face at the mention of Fat Louie and then my "sugar momma grandma" had turned into a gargoyle's rictus grin the moment Boris had uttered Michael's ex-girlfriend's name. But I couldn't help it. That's a name I hadn't heard in a long time. Since high school, as a matter of fact. It's a name I'd hoped never to hear again, and yet here I was, on the sunniest of days in beautiful Genovia, more than a decade after high school graduation, hearing it again. "Judith? Do you mean *Judith Gershner*?"

"Yeah, Judith," he said. Boris seemed to be feeling much better now that he'd already downed about half the bottle of champagne. "Michael was telling me the vaccine is in clinical trials now. That's so cool. You must be so proud of him."

"I am. Very proud." My grin was practically splitting my face in two. "But what about Judith Gershner again?"

"Just that who'd ever have guessed that old Judith Gershner would turn out to be an award-winning geneticist who'd be helping Michael, the Prince of Genovia, with his intranasal vaccine against COVID? That is just so great. Life's funny, isn't it? Boy, am I glad I came here. Oh, I'm sorry, I never offered you any of this great champagne. Want some? Mia? Mia, are you all right?"

No. No, I was most definitely not all right.

Excuse me. But what?

What???

WHAT??????????????

Everything is normal. Everything is fine.

Boris is right. Michael and I are the perfect couple.

Just because Michael's been gone almost every single day, all day, for this entire pandemic, working on his intranasal vaccine in his lab, and never once thought to mention that his *ex-girlfriend is working on it with him* does NOT mean he is cheating on me, because Michael Moscovitz would never, ever do that.

Where would he even find the *time* to do that? When he's not at his lab he's back home with me and the twins, who, he's said on multiple occasions, are the loves of his life—right after me, the most important love of his life.

He told me just the other day that he cannot even envision life without me.

Granted, this was as we were sharing a bowl

of chocolate mousse while watching a *Law & Order: SVU* marathon.

And granted, his exact words were, "I'm so glad you put that minifridge in here, Mia. It makes eating mousse in bed while watching *SVU* so much more convenient. You are a most excellent wife."

But still. It's basically the same thing as saying that his heart burns only for me and that he would sooner die than be with any other woman, including Olivia Benson.

So he absolutely cannot be having an affair with Judith Gershner.

But then why did he mention to BORIS PELKOWSKI and NOT ME that he's collaborating on his intranasal vaccine with Judith???

Obviously after I left Boris—who was dialing Tina's number and then crooning, "Tee? Tee, it's me. Baby, please call me back. I am the biggest, stupidest idiot in the entire world and I will do anything, anything at all to get you back"—I took out my own phone and FaceTimed Michael to find out what the hell was going on.

Only he did not pick up.

Of course there are a thousand reasons he might not have picked up. He could have been:

- In a meeting

- Giving an interview to CNN about his amazing, life-saving vaccine

- At his office gym, working out to keep those amazing, young Elliot Stabler–like muscles of his in shape

- At a very important lunch with very important world leaders who are hoping to procure his lifesaving vaccine for themselves to distribute to their own people

It's extremely unlikely that he was at that lunch or meeting with Judith Gershner, or that he and Judith were making wild, passionate scientist love on top of one of their desks. I don't know why I even allowed that thought to manifest itself in my brain.

But it did, so much so that when I wandered back to the pool area, Lana looked up from the chaise lounge upon which she was still stretched out, looking at the pictures in the latest copy of French *Vogue*, and gasped.

"Mia, what's the matter? Did Fat Louie eat another sock?"

"No," I said, and collapsed onto the empty chaise beside her. Fortunately I didn't have to worry about any of the others overhearing us because they'd all retired to the terrace to have lunch—except for Grandmère, who'd taken off for the yacht club for her weekly confab with her fellow InFLUENZers. "Lana, can you look something up for me on social media?"

Lana's eyes widened behind the lenses of her Chanel sunglasses. "Of course! Is it hot goss? You know how much I love sizzling hot goss! Did something happen with Meghan and Harry?"

"No," I said, feeling ill. "It's not about Meghan and Harry. But it is 100 percent hot goss. Could you please look up the name Judith Gershner?"

By this time Lilly had come down to the pool from her office over in the East Wing. She paused on her way to the lunch table to stare at me.

"Mia," she said. "Why do you want to know what's going on with my brother's ex-girlfriend?"

Lana wrinkled her nose in disgust as her thumbs flew across her phone's screen. "Ew. You don't mean that same Judith Gershner who we went to high school with, do you, Mia? Wasn't she that ugly girl who cloned a house fly or whatever it was, and won the science fair, which by rights I should have won?"

"It was the Biomedical Technology Fair," I said. "And it was a fruit fly, and I don't recall you ever even entering the Biomedical Technology Fair, Lana. And Judith wasn't a bit ugly. She had raven curls and creamy skin and none of the boys could resist her."

Lana snorted. "That's totally the opposite of how I remember it. The only boy who I recall liking Judith was Michael. And even then he only liked her because she had those really big—"

"Just do it, Lana," I said.

"—*books*, I was going to say." Lana rolled her

eyes. "She was always lugging around those huge science books in that equally huge backpack. Anyway, here she is. This has to be the same girl. Er, woman." Lana read aloud from her phone. "Judith Gershner, BS in microbiology from Columbia, MS and PhD from Harvard Medical School's Blavatnik Institute of Genetics—God, who puts all of this in their Twitter bio? Why doesn't she put in anything about how much she enjoys pumpkin spice lattes, like a normal—"

"Okay, okay." I felt my stomach lurch. "That's enough." How many advanced degrees from Ivy League universities could one person have?

"Are those horn-rimmed glasses supposed to be ironic?" Lana held up her phone to show me Judith's profile pic. "And what's with her hair? I don't remember her being Amish."

"Lana." Lilly pointed at her own glasses. "Remember when we had that talk about how you were not going to judge women by their appearance because it's sexist and wrong, and that society's standards of beauty for women are incredibly unrealistic, and you wanted to set a good example for your daughter?"

Lana lowered her phone with a pout. "Sorry, you're right. But Judith honestly needs my help. With a little styling gel and an introduction to my plastic surgeon, she could actually be—"

"Why this sudden interest in Judith Gershner after all these years, Mia?" Lilly demanded. Her voice, like her gaze, was sharp.

I sighed. I knew I was going to have to come clean sometime, especially if Michael and I got divorced. I would be forced to pay him alimony, and we'd have to split custody of the kids. I would take Elizabeth and Michael would take Frank, *Parent Trap*–style. As my royal sister-in-law, Lilly would be bound to notice.

"Boris just got here," I said, nodding my head toward the Rose Garden. "He flew in because he wanted some advice on how to get Tina to take him back."

"Oh!" Lana picked up her copy of French *Vogue* and waved it. "That's so romantic! Where is he? Tell him to come over here. I've got so many apology gift ideas for him. I just saw the L'Heure du Diamant collection at Chopard and I think Tina would *love* their ethical diamond heart necklace set in platinum—"

"I don't want to disturb him," I said. I was pretty sure Tina had matured to a point where it was going to take way more than an ethical diamond heart necklace to get her to forgive Boris. "He's trying to call her now."

"Oh, well, when he hangs up, then," Lana said. "We can go shopping together later this afternoon! I just know the necklace will do it. Boris and Tina are such a cute couple, like you and Michael."

Like Michael and I used to be, I thought, *before he started keeping secrets, like his geneticist mistress, from me.*

But it made sense. How could I, someone who didn't even listen to him when he started going on about what RNA was, compete with someone who not only knew, but had so many degrees in it?

"I don't understand what Boris being here has to do with Judith Gershner," Lilly declared.

"Yes," I said. "Well, I asked Michael to speak to Boris about the whole Tina thing. You remember how Boris is very good at music, but sometimes needs a little help with showing simple human empathy?" Both Lilly and Lana nodded knowingly. "Well, Boris just told me that while Michael was talking to him, he mentioned that Judith's been collaborating with him on his vaccine trial."

Both Lana and Lilly continued to stare at me expectantly.

"*And?*" Lilly prompted, when I didn't continue.

"And," I cried, frustrated. "And that's it. *Judith Gershner's* been working with Michael on his vaccine trial this whole time. This *whole time*! And Michael's never mentioned it to me."

Lana looked confused. "Well, why would he tell you that this boring woman is working with him?" she asked. "You should be thankful he didn't. You don't know how many times I've had to ask Jason to please leave his work stuff back at the office where it belongs. I don't want that dark energy around the children. I try to keep our home a place of positivity and light."

"Lana," I said, fighting for patience. *"Judith Gershner is Michael's ex-girlfriend."*

"So?" Lana took a long slurp of the champagne she'd set on the table beside her chaise lounge. Then, as the reality of what I was implying set in, her eyes widened, and she started laughing. "Wait a minute. You can't . . . you don't . . ."

"She does." Lilly was shaking her head. "She completely does."

"But." Lana showed me Judith's profile pic again. "How could you possibly think Michael is having an affair with *her*? She looks like Angela Merkel."

"Lana," Lilly said in a warning voice. "Remember what I told you?"

"Yes," Lana said. "Of course. But honestly. It's true you've really let yourself go lately, Mia, with the cardigans and the yoga pants and whatever is going on with your hair. But you still look better than *Judith Gershner.*"

I'd had about all I could take when it came to unwelcome houseguests sharing their opinions.

"Do you even know my husband *at all*, Lana?" I demanded. "Because if you did, you would know that he is a man who is attracted to people because of their intelligence, humor, and compassion, *not* their looks."

"Okay, Jane Eyre," Lilly said, patting me on the shoulder. "Calm down. Michael isn't having an affair with Judith Gershner."

"How do you know?" I was doing my best not

to burst into tears, but it wasn't easy. I'd managed to make it through nearly a year of COVID without weeping, but this, on top of how ungrateful certain members of my family were being for all my hard work, was the final straw.

And it wasn't because of mild cognitive impairment, or even PMS, either. After the "surprise" (not accident, because accidents are bad. Surprises are good) that had caused the twins, I've been really good about taking my birth control pills, which are the year-round kind where you never get a period, because princesses are busy and don't have time for menstruation—which, as my mother likes to point out, now that modern medicine exists, is only a tool of the patriarchy to keep women oppressed. Regular monthly periods don't provide any health benefits, and with the birth control pill, are no longer necessary.

So it wasn't as if I was suffering from PMS. What I was feeling was pure, unadulterated rage, mixed with frustration and sorrow.

"How do you know, Lilly?" I asked, not bothering to blink back my tears. "How do you know your brother isn't having an affair?"

"Well, for one thing," Lilly said, "because I know Michael, and he's strictly a one-woman-at-a-time kind of man. He wouldn't know how to handle more than one woman at once, believe me. And for another, he's been in love with you and only you, Mia, for as long as I can remember. And for a third, it would be kind of hard for

Judith and Michael to have an affair considering the fact that *they don't even live in the same country.*"

"That's right." Lana was reading from her phone. "It says here that Judith lives in Cambridge, Massachusetts, with her husband and five children, whom she's currently homeschooling while also working at the Broad Institute of Harvard and MIT in biomedical and genomic research."

I became blinded by my tears. "She's a geneticist at Harvard *who still finds time to homeschool her five kids?*" I could barely handle two toddlers with the help of my husband, my mother, my sister-in-law, and a full palace staff, let alone also run a country with the help of Parliament and a prime minister.

"Oh," Lana said. "Sorry. Her husband, Collin, is a novelist, and he homeschools the children because it's important to him and Judith that they spend as much time as possible together as a family. Judith's also a part-time rabbi. She works with bar and bat mitzvah candidates to help them fulfill their true potential."

I flopped back against the chaise lounge. "I'm going to kill myself."

"Oh, don't be so dramatic, Mia." Lana rolled her eyes. "Judith's not so great. See, she posted right here that her kids are all under the age of ten but reading at a ninth-grade level already."

"How is that not so great?" I asked, bewildered.

Lana shrugged. "It's easy to homeschool geniuses. She and Collin should try homeschooling a kid like Rocky. That'd be a real accomplishment."

I thought about wrapping my arms around one of the marble busts of my ancestors and throwing it and myself into the deep end of the pool.

"Lana, shut up." Lilly shook me by the arm. "See, Mia? This is why you don't have social media. It only gives you feelings of inferiority when you're actually doing great, even if you don't have any advanced degrees or homeschool anyone. Now why don't we go have some lunch? I think your blood sugar might be a little low."

"No." I sat up and wrenched my arm from her grasp. "I'm going to Michael's lab, and I'm going to ask him myself about Judith."

"You can't go out," Lilly said. "There are armed men at the palace gates."

Lana sprang from her chaise lounge and began wriggling into her beach cover-up. "Ooooh, if you're going out, can I go, too? We haven't gone out *once* the entire time I've been here. I'm going stir-crazy. And I want to stop by Jewels of Genovia to see if they have any of those diamond necklaces for Boris to buy for Tina. I want Jason to buy one for me. He still owes me a push present for Sir Jason Junior."

Lilly sent Lana a scathing look. "Are you serious? Isn't the reward for giving birth that you get a *baby*?"

"Um, get back to me after you've pushed a ten-pound bowling ball with fingernails out of your vagina, Lilly," Lana shot back.

"Neither of you are coming with me." I began making my way back toward the Rose Garden, and the palace gates. "I have to do this on my own."

But of course my friends wouldn't let me do it on my own. For one thing because they're good friends who wanted to help me, and for another, because I actually needed that help—in more ways than one.

"Uh, do you really think it's the best idea to leave without any sort of plan when René and his friends are out there, waiting to arrest you?" Lilly asked as she trotted after me. "Especially when you could be so easily recognized? Your profile is plastered all over the money in this country."

"I don't think anyone is going to recognize her," Lana sniffed, "considering the fact that she doesn't look anything like Princess Amelia of Genovia."

I glared at her. "What are you talking about?"

"Well, the Princess of Genovia that *I* know wouldn't be caught dead going to rescue her marriage from a home-wrecking Harvard geneticist in sweatpants and a Spice Girls concert T-shirt—and especially not with three inches of gray roots showing in her hair."

"Lana," Lilly said in a warning voice, but I held up a hand to stop her. I could fight my own battles.

"For your information, Lana," I said, "I *earned* every one of these gray hairs dealing with the stress of the pandemic. If you think I'm going to call Paolo to have them covered up when I'm actually *proud* of them, you're nuts. And the Spice Girls are feminist icons."

Lana looked dubious. "Okay. But those sweatpants you're wearing?"

"I need to be able to move freely." I didn't want to admit that thanks to my excessive steak frites and wine consumption, the sweatpants were the only clothes I owned that still fit, aside from my maternity wear. "Lilly's right. We're living in a war zone, practically."

"Exactly why Lars is never going to let you order a limo to be driven out of here." Lilly shook her head at me. "Can't you just wait until Michael gets home?"

But how was I going to catch Michael in the act of making wild, passionate scientist love on a desk to Judith Gershner if I waited until he got home? Not that the rational part of my brain believed this was actually happening.

But the irrational part that had broken down due to the stress of the pandemic and too many idiotic houseguests and family members did believe it. Why else had he never mentioned her to me?

"No," I said, and then called out to Boris, who was still sitting on the marble bench where I'd left him, his head bent over his phone as he texted furiously into it. He looked up at us, surprised when he heard his name.

"Oh, hey," he said, brightening. "I still can't get ahold of—*Lana?* What are *you* doing here?"

"Hi, Boris." Lana sounded about as thrilled to see him as he looked confused to see her. "Lilly and I are just trying to keep Mia from making the biggest mistake of her life."

"Zip it, Lana," I said. "Boris, did you rent a car to get here from the airport, or take a taxi?"

"I got a car from Genovia Luxury Rentals." He stood up and puffed out his chest a little, like he always did when Lilly was around, even though the two of them had broken up more than a decade ago and moved on to other people. "I wanted a Bugatti, but they were all taken by tourists. The only thing they had left was a Maserati Quattroporte. It's not as cool, of course, but I said I'd take it because the alternative was to—"

"Great, great," I said. I had no idea what he was talking about. All I knew was that he had a car. "Give me the keys. I need to borrow it to go downtown to Michael's office."

"Okay." He tucked his phone into a pocket of his leather pants. I was surprised it could fit, considering how tight they were, but somehow he managed to pry a set of car keys from them, as well, and hand them to me. I tried not to freak out by how warm they felt. "I need to talk to Michael myself. Tina's not picking up or answering my texts. Maybe he'll have some tips on what I can say to get through to her."

"She's probably asleep." Lilly's voice was cutting. "It's six o'clock in the morning in New York right now. And Mia's not going anywhere." To me, she said, "Have you lost your mind? You're not going downtown with *Boris*."

"I most certainly am."

"Well, you're not letting him drive in his condition."

I dangled the car keys. "I'm driving."

"You don't even have a license." She tried to snatch the keys away from me, but I pulled them from her reach. "Mia," she said, glaring at me. "As your personal attorney, sister-in-law, and best friend, I'm advising you not to go anywhere near those gates."

Lana looked outraged. "I thought *I* was Mia's best friend."

"I'm going to see Michael," I hissed at Lilly through gritted teeth. "And I'm taking Boris's stupid luxury rental car since neither the press nor the protesters will realize I'm in it, since I normally only in travel in zero emission limos and I apparently look like some hideous beast now and not my normal self." I glared at Lana, who blinked uncomprehendingly back at me. "Now, either you're coming with me, or you're getting out of my way."

Which is how Boris, Lilly, Lana, and I ended

up here, squeezed into Boris's luxury rental car. Fortunately the car has tinted windows, so no one at the palace gates saw me huddled here in the back seat, let alone recognized me. No one, of course, except the Genovian guards, who saw me climbing into the car in the first place, and alerted Lars immediately about what I was trying to do.

That's why I'm stuck here in the back seat between him and Lana, because of course he insisted on coming along to Michael's office as well.

He didn't try to talk me out of going, though. He did lift both eyebrows when I told him why I was making the trip—because I suspected Michael was having an affair.

"Michael?" Lars looked baffled. "Your husband, Michael?"

"Don't act like you don't know what I'm talking about!" I snatched Lana's phone from her hands and showed him Judith's profile pic. "They've been working on the vaccine together this whole time!"

Lars lifted his Ray-Bans and stooped to study the photo. "I do not know this man."

"Ha!" Lana clapped her hands in delight. "Ha, ha, ha!"

"That is a woman, and you know it, Lars." I glared at him. "And you recognize her, too."

I think he recognized by the wild look in my eyes that I was a woman who'd been pushed to the brink of her sanity by her own friends and family—not to mention one of the deadliest pandemics in recorded history—since he said only, "If you say so, Your Highness," and folded himself into the back seat beside me.

But this is my life now, I guess. Even though we're living during a time of unprecedented loneliness and isolation, I will probably never again get a minute to myself.

"Really?" Lana just sneered in a very amused voice, because she read the line I wrote above about not seeming to get a minute to myself (she couldn't help it, since we're squeezed in here so tightly, my elbow keeps bumping her as I write, and also Lilly is a very aggressive driver. There is so much traffic on the road because there are so many tourists driving their own stupid luxury rental vehicles—not to mention Uber drivers—that it's difficult to get anywhere quickly anymore).

BUT ANYWAY: YES, LANA, THIS IS MY LIFE NOW. THIS IS ALL OF OUR LIVES NOW, THANKS TO COVID. NOTHING WILL EVER BE THE SAME. WE WILL FOREVER BE—

Oh, never mind. We just pulled up in front of Michael's building.

*B*oris, as oblivious as always to social cues, tried to come with me to "say hello" to Michael.

I told him that he had to stay in the car with Lilly and Lana, who cried, "Boris, what are you doing? Get back in here. You're supposed to come with me to Jewels of Genovia to help me pick out my push present. I mean, let me help you pick out something for Tina that will make her get back together with you."

"Oh," Boris said. He slipped back into his seat. "Thanks, Lana."

"Good luck saving your marriage, Mia!" Lilly waved from behind the wheel as she drove away, and Lars and I strode across the underground parking garage beneath the building in which Pavlov Surgical is housed (on the top floor, above many offices belonging to plastic surgeons and "wellness" practitioners).

I was too busy glaring at Lilly over my shoulder to notice the well-dressed masked man who was standing at the garage elevator, a couple boxes of pizza from V.I.P.'s in his hands, until I'd almost bumped into him. When I did, I was surprised to hear him say, "Mia?"

His voice sounded very familiar. I looked up. *"Michael?"*

"Hey!" Michael grinned broadly at us (even though he was masked, I could tell by his floppy hair and the way the skin around his eyes crinkled), then leaned down to kiss me on the cheek. "What are you doing here? You didn't say you'd be stopping by my office today."

"No." I was confused. He looked delighted to see me, and not at all like someone who'd been caught having an illicit affair with his geneticist ex-girlfriend. "Lars and I were just in the area because, uh—"

"You remembered! Oh, wow, this is great!" Michael pressed the up button on the elevator with his elbow. "Everybody's going to be so excited to see you! A visit from the Princess of Genovia? This will be such a morale booster for them, you have no idea. Especially today."

"T-today?"

"Yes! I can't believe you remembered!"

I stole a glance at Lars, but he looked as bewildered as I felt. "Of . . . of course I remembered. How could I forget?"

What had I forgotten? It had to be something important in order for Michael to look so happy that I'd remembered.

But who could remember anything during these chaotic times? Especially when there were two-year-olds in the house, plus constantly vomiting house pets and my grandmother.

I cast around desperately for some small clue as to what Michael might be talking about, but the only thing that registered was the pizzas he was holding.

"So," I said, because I literally could think of nothing else. I think my brain was numb from all the information Lana had read to me from her phone. "Pizza, huh?"

"Yes! I know it's dumb, but the staff loves the pizza from V.I.P.'s, and I really wanted to make today special for them, you know? Probably I should have ordered a cake, but who wouldn't prefer pizza to cake when their vaccine passes its final trial phase?"

"Right. Right, of course!"

This was not going at all the way I'd planned.

Not that I'd done any actual planning, because when you're seized with pandemic-induced hysteria that your partner is having an affair, you don't really plan much of anything.

But I certainly hadn't anticipated Michael being happy to see me, much less celebrating the completion of the final phase of his vaccine trial.

"Um," I said. "I tried calling, but you didn't pick up."

"Did you?" He handed me the pizzas so that he could dig into the pocket of his nicely fitting gray cords and pulled out his phone. "Oh, so you did! I didn't hear it ring. It was a zoo at V.I.P.'s. I called in my order over an hour ago and then they got slammed by tourists ordering pizza-by-the-slice and couldn't spare anyone to deliver." He shoved his phone back in his pocket and took the boxes from me again with a smile. "But now I'm glad I did, since I got to run into you."

The elevator dinged, and then the doors slid open. Michael held them for us. "After you, Your Highness," he said to me.

"Why, thank you, Your Highness." I stepped onto the elevator, followed by Lars, and tried to tamp down the crushing anxiety I was feeling over the fact that I hadn't listened to Lilly's advice and simply stayed at the palace and waited for Michael to come home. Now I was heading up to his office—a place I hadn't been to since I'd cut the ribbon at its grand opening, back when none of us had to wear face masks and my hair hadn't been full of gray streaks.

Not that I cared how I looked. I'd been telling the truth when I'd told Lana that I thought the Spice Girls were feminist icons.

But I did very much wish I had at least changed out of my sweatpants and into something slightly more flattering before making this unannounced visit during what was apparently a happy day of celebration.

It was too late, though. When the elevator doors slid open again, we were on the building's top floor—and immediately plunged into the high-tech steel-and-glass world of Pavlov Surgical. There were smart-looking people everywhere in lab coats and rectangularly framed glasses, one of whom stopped midstride upon seeing us and cried, "Hey, Moscovitz is back! With pizza, everyone!"

"Pizza party!" shouted someone else.

Well. It was certainly nice to know that Michael wasn't given any special treatment by his colleagues just because he was prince consort to their royal princess.

"You deserve it," Michael said as he placed the pizzas on the receptionist's desk. "Couldn't have done it without all of you. And look who stopped by to express her appreciation as well!"

Michael gestured toward me with a look of such total adoration and pride that I felt an instant rush of shame. It was 100 percent obvious in that moment that:

1. He was absolutely delighted to see me, and thrilled to show me off to his colleagues.

2. He was not having an affair with anyone, let alone Judith Gershner.

3. I was the biggest idiot in the world. And yet for some reason, Michael hadn't realized it yet, and still wanted to stay married to me.

All of the scientists and lab technicians who'd come rushing to the reception area to grab slices of pizza said enthusiastic hellos to me as they pulled down their masks and chowed down on their lunch (don't ask me why they chose to eat their pizza in the reception area instead of the nice dining/kitchen area I happened to know was in the back, since I'd helped pay for it) except for one young female scientist (who was most definitely not Judith Gershner). She froze midbite, her eyes widening as she stared at me.

"Oh . . . my . . . God," she murmured. "Aren't you . . . aren't you . . . *are* you . . . ?"

Everyone else stopped eating as well, their gazes flicking toward me curiously, except of course for Lars, who looked mildly amused behind his face mask.

Michael, however, appeared delighted. "Yes," he cried. "It's Princess Mia. She stopped by to say thanks and great job, everyone!"

"Oh . . ." The young female scientist glanced from me to the portrait of me hanging above the reception desk (there are portraits of me hanging above reception desks all over Genovia. I don't understand why, but wherever mail is received in Genovia, you'll find a portrait of me. Possibly this is to remind people to use correct postage, since my face is also on most of the stamps?), and then back again. She looked mortified. "I'm so sorry, Your Highness. We, er, didn't recognize you."

"No, of course you didn't." I could practically feel the embarrassment radiating from her. "It's so difficult these days, isn't it, with all of us in masks?"

"Ha, ha," she said, with a nervous glance at her colleagues. "Yes. Yes, it is!"

But of course I knew it wasn't only the mask. I pushed self-consciously at my bangs, which were supposed to swoop sexily down in front of one of my eyes, but lately sort of frame both sides of my face like a thick curtain since I haven't allowed Paolo near me in so long—not because I'm afraid I'll catch COVID from him, but because I've gotten used to going "au naturel." This months-long break from having to have my hair blown out every day (and dressing in business suits, and having to shake a zillion strangers' hands) has been such a restful change of pace.

But now I could tell that perhaps Lana had been right after all, and I'd let things go a little too far—at least judging from the fact that no one at Michael's lab could recognize me. I no longer looked like the perfect, polished princess in the portrait above my people's reception desk, or on their money or stamps.

But had I *ever* been that perfect, polished princess?

I cleared my throat and said, "I came here today to say thank you so much for all the important work you're doing on what will be Europe's— and possibly the world's—first intranasal COVID vaccine. You can't imagine how proud the prime minister and I are of all of you. You are true heroes in our eyes. Thank you, thank you so much."

There. How did that sound? Good, I thought—at least judging by the way they'd stopped chewing their pizza and were looking around at one another with obvious delight.

Obviously I'd had to lie since I couldn't tell them why I'd *really* stopped by.

But I could see with my own eyes that Judith Gershner was nowhere on the premises. And also that Michael was bursting with pride over his workplace and colleagues, and with excitement that I'd taken the time to visit, even if it wasn't for the reason he thought.

"Let me give you a tour!" Michael cried, grabbing my hand and dragging me through the reception area and back toward the actual lab. "You haven't been here in a while."

And that's how I ended up hearing all about CRISPR gene editing, inert protein subunits, and something called "negative interference from anti-vector antibodies."

I'm pretending like I'm taking notes—and I suppose I am, in a way. It's actually very nice to be around so many people who love their jobs so much, and who are of course doing something so important. I even see now why they eat their lunch in the reception area as opposed to the lovely dining/kitchen room (which has a beautiful outdoor patio with a Zen garden and meditation fountain) I had designed for them: it's so important that they get this vaccine rolled out next month, they don't have time to sit down for a lunch.

The scientists were telling me all about how they're hoping vaccine rollout will occur (health-care and frontline workers and senior citizens will receive the first doses: I can only imagine what Grandmère will have to say about that) when there was a chiming sound. That was when one of Michael's colleagues cried, "Oh, that's them," all excitedly.

Then, above our heads, a large monitor flickered to life, and suddenly I was looking at a half dozen other scientists' faces, apparently from America, one of whom looked uncannily like . . .

Judith Gershner.

"Hello, there," Michael said, cheerfully enough—but he did not look even an eighth as excited to see Judith as he'd been when he'd first seen me downstairs in the parking garage. "Thank you for joining us, doctors! Mia, you remember Judith, don't you? She's been working on the vaccine with us. Judith, you remember Mia, right?"

Judith in real life looked about as much like her profile picture as I looked like my royal portrait. She still had raven hair, but there was a bright white streak just like mine running all the way down her center part, and her pale creamy skin was dotted with red spots of an indeterminate origin—at least until the face of a small child that looked very much like her appeared over her shoulder and screamed, "Is it time for the MEET-ING, Mom?"

Then I saw that he (or she) had similar spots all over his (or her) face.

"Oh, hello, Mia," Judith said in a voice that sounded warm but very tired. "It's so good to see you." She was trying to push away not just the child that was asking if it was time for the meeting, but another child that had appeared—also covered in red spots—waving a book (that did not appear to be ninth-grade reading level since it had large pictures), crying, "Mommy, Mommy, read this to me!"

"You'll have to excuse me," Judith said. "We're having a slight parvovirus outbreak here at the moment, which is why I'm working from home today. But it's lovely to see you, Your Highness. You look as beautiful and glamorous as ever."

I had no idea what she was talking about, since I knew I looked about as beautiful and glamorous as she did.

But I played along, smiling (beneath my mask) and saying, "Thank you. And thank you so much for all the help I understand you've been giving us on this vaccine."

"Yes," Michael said. He was looking at me with as much adoration as Prince Albert had looked at Queen Victoria in the movie *The Young Victoria*, when they'd worked together to modernize Great Britain and bring it peaceful prosperity.

"Without this partnership, we might never have made this happen. But because of it, we should be the first country in the EU to have a safe and effective intranasal vaccine ready before Christmas."

All the scientists began to cheer.

"Well," I said. "That is such great news. I'm so happy to hear it. And I do hope you feel better soon, Dr. Gershner."

"Oh, please," she said modestly. "Call me Judith!"

Then one of Judith Gershner's five children threw something at the monitor and we lost the connection, so while Pavlov Surgical's IT team struggled to get it back, I took the opportunity to say to Michael, in the sweetest voice I could summon, "You never told me you were working on your intranasal vaccine with Judith Gershner."

Michael looked up from the pizza he was attacking—he'd been so busy showing me around, he hadn't gotten to eat lunch. "Yes, I did."

I fought for inner patience. "No, Michael. You did not."

He smiled at me with the same fondness I often caught him smiling at the children with when they were doing or saying boneheaded things. "Yes, Mia, I did. Dozens of times. You just never listen because you're too caught up in your own work or family drama. It's okay—I completely get it. But it's true."

"Michael." I lowered my voice so that no one,

not even Lars, would overhear me. "There is no way on God's green earth that if you'd told me you were working on your intranasal vaccine with your EX-GIRLFRIEND, JUDITH GERSHNER, that I would not have noticed. I had to hear it from Boris Pelkowski, of all people."

"Boris?" Michael looked curious. "What's Boris got to do with all this?"

"Boris showed up at the palace this morning."

Michael looked amused. "Oh, right! What she want?"

"Well, he took your advice and tried to speak to Tina, but she won't see him or take his calls. So he wanted to get more tips. He's over at Jewels of Genovia right now with your sister and Lana, looking for apology gifts."

"For us? He's welcome to stay with us anytime, isn't he? He doesn't have to buy us apology gifts."

May God have mercy on my soul. "No. Not for us. For Tina!"

Michael rolled his eyes. "Typical Boris."

"I know. But that is not the point. The point, Michael, is that you never mentioned you were working with Judith!"

Michael grinned at me. "Oh my God. You're jealous."

"I am not!"

"Yes, you are. You're jealous of Judith Gershner."

"I am NOT jealous of Judith Gershner."

"You're jealous of a woman I haven't seen in

person in fifteen years, who has five kids, parvo-virus, and lives four thousand miles away."

"I am NOT jealous of her. I just think it's very suspicious that you never once mentioned to me that you were working with her on this project—"

Michael snaked an arm around my waist and pulled me up against him. "I like it when you're jealous."

"Michael!" I looked around, certain that all of his colleagues were staring at us.

But they weren't. They'd returned to their workstations, because when you're working against the clock to make a lifesaving vaccine, you don't have time for two-hour pizza parties. Even Lars had picked up a copy of *Genovian Health Today* from the coffee table in the lobby and wandered away with it somewhere.

Still, even though we were alone, I was shocked when Michael pulled down my face mask and kissed me—and not the quick, teasing kiss I was expecting, either. Maybe that was what he'd been intending at first, but it soon turned into some-thing much, much more . . .

. . . at least until Lars came wandering back from wherever he'd been, looked up from his copy of *Genovian Health*, and cried, "Oh, excuse me, Your Highnesses!"

Michael did not appear the least bit perturbed. In fact, he was laughing.

"Lars," he said, while I was practically throwing myself behind a high-tech couch in shame. "Did

I or did I not mention in front of Mia on multiple occasions that Judith Gershner was working with me on this vaccine project?"

Lars nodded. "You did."

I couldn't believe it. "You are both gaslighting me."

"You're the mother of young children," Lars said. "And you've got elderly relatives at home as well. You're part of the sandwich generation." He waved his copy of *Genovian Health* to reveal where he'd gotten this information. "It's to be expected that you're going to let a few things slip through the cracks."

"Yeah," Michael said to me. "Don't be so hard on yourself. Be thankful it's just Judith Gershner. It could have been something much worse."

Am I wrong not to feel at all comforted by their words? Because in spite of the fact that I've seen today that a vaccine is on its way, I think something worse is still to come.

Quarantine Day After

*T*he something worse came.

I just didn't think it would be so soon.

Obviously I was in a celebratory mood upon returning home to the palace. Who wouldn't have been after the morning I'd had? I'd gone from the depths of despair—thinking my husband was having an affair with his geneticist ex-girlfriend—to the heights of giddy ecstasy. Michael was not only *not* having an affair with his ex, but he loved me more than ever *and* was finished making a vaccine that we could now release to the public . . . well, to the elderly and our nation's health-care and frontline workers, but eventually to everyone, thus saving thousands of lives . . .

Genovian lives, anyway. I cannot be responsible for the lives of anyone else. One can take on only so much. That's something I've learned during my time as a royal: you can't save *everyone*. You can only save the people who want to be saved, and sometimes not even all of them. Some people simply won't allow themselves to be saved. Even when you're standing there in front of them, holding a life jacket and saying, "*This. This* will save you," they still won't put it on, usually because they saw some forty-five-minute YouTube video produced by a chiropractor in New Jersey who claims that in some non–peer reviewed study they once read, life jackets can sometimes be unsafe, or something like that.

Anyway. As we drove back to the palace from Michael's office—Michael left with us, following in his own car—I began finally to feel as if everything might actually be all right. All the stress that had settled between my shoulders that I hadn't been able to get rid of (because you can't have a massage during a pandemic as that violates social distancing) was beginning to melt away. Melt away because, thanks to Michael and his miracle vaccine, there was a chance everything was going to be okay.

Okay? Everything was going to be *great*. Everything was going to be better than great. Everything was going to be *normal* again.

At least that's what I was thinking as we whizzed by the crowded casinos and luxury shops and outdoor cafés and restaurants (Lars refused to allow Lilly to drive us home, so our route back to the palace was much faster and filled with less braking, but of course more cursing at masked tourists who'd wandered out into the middle of the road for selfies, because Lars has no patience for that kind of thing).

I was beaming about how normal everything was going to be again soon all the way up to the palace's front gates, where my cousin René and his idiot friends once again didn't recognize me in the back seat of Boris's rental car—although I did notice that there were fewer of them. Was René's protest losing some of its steam? I hoped so! Soon there wouldn't be any of them, because Michael's vaccine would be available and we wouldn't need masks and they could all go home, even René.

I floated on my happy cloud about it as Michael and I followed Lana through the Great Hall toward the pool where our babies were paddling around with Purple Iris, Sir Jason Junior and their father, who did not look very enthused by Lana's shriek of, "Oh my God, Jason, you should see what you bought me! It cost so much money! But I deserve it."

I was still enveloped in its pink warmth while Michael and I watched Boris show Jason the new ten-carat cruelty-free diamond engagement ring he'd bought for Tina, to whom—Boris said—he intended to re-propose as soon as he got back to New York.

"And," Boris told us all, happily, "I'm going to sell the house in Malibu and buy a house in the Hamptons. Because if you love someone, you have to support their dreams, and Tina's dream is to be a doctor in New York City. I can be a musician anywhere."

"That is so romantic," Lana said with a sigh. All of us, it seemed, were wrapped in the same cloud of joy. "Jason, I have an idea. Let's support Boris by buying the beach house in Malibu from him. Haven't you always wanted one?"

"No," Jason said, who by this time had gotten out of the pool to pour himself a whiskey, probably in order to help himself through the sticker shock of the push present Lana had purchased for herself.

It was at this precise moment that our radiant cloud of hope burst, and everything went to s***, as my children would put it. Because it was at this precise moment that Grandmère returned from the yacht club.

Everything seemed all right, at first. She was in her usual fine form, dressed in the height of Genovian chic: a white sun hat with a massive brim, purple sunglasses with frames that were far too large for her face, and a mauve jumpsuit coupled with a flowing white scarf that trailed several feet behind her. Her painted-on eyebrows were sharply defined as if freshly applied, and Rommel was shivering as usual in her arms.

"*Bonjour, mes chéris,*" she greeted us cheerfully as she strode onto the terrace. "How are you on this gorgeous afternoon?"

"Great," Lana said, and waved her arm so Grandmère would be sure to notice the expensive diamond bracelet dangling from her wrist (she had decided the heart necklace wasn't right for her).

"Oh, isn't that lovely?" Grandmère bent her

regal neck to examine the jewels. "Jewels of Genovia?"

"Yes!" Lana cooed.

Of course Grandmère could tell, without even putting on her readers, the exact place Lana had acquired her latest prize.

"An excellent choice." Grandmère glanced from Lana's wrist to the pool, where Michael and I had joined the children. "And where are the other young people?"

By "other young people" she meant her fiancé, Derek, which of course was disturbing, but I'd given up thinking too much about my grandmother's sex life, because otherwise my head would go spinning off into the stratosphere.

"Niamh usually has class right about now," Jason replied unhelpfully, because of course Grandmère didn't mean Niamh. "Zoom tap dancing, I think? And Khalil and Olivia said they had class, too. And Prince Phillipe and Helen went to go check on the renovation at the summer palace."

"And Derek?" Grandmère asked. She'd spied a footperson and jiggled her hand in the air, her universally understood gesture for "please bring me a Sidecar." The footperson bowed and scurried off to do so.

Derek's schedule Jason knew. "I think he's in the pool house playing *Call of Duty* with Chad and Rocky," he said. He started to rise from his chaise lounge. "Speaking of which, I might join th—"

"Oh, don't get up." Grandmère waved the

brightly colored paper bag she was holding, on which the ornately scrolled initials *YC* were stamped. "I brought Derek his favorite dessert, the white chocolate mousse, from the club as a surprise. I'll just take it into him. I'll only be a moment."

"But Gwandmewair," Iris shrieked from the water. "I'm about to do a somersault. Look! LOOK!"

Grandmère was, to Purple Iris, basically the most glamorous person in the entire world—outside of Princess Olivia, of course. But since Olivia was busy with her schoolwork, Grandmère would have to do.

"I will be happy to watch you do a dozen somersaults, *ma petite*," Grandmère said, as she clip-clopped toward the pool house in her heels. "Just as soon as I return from this important errand."

Both Iris and her father looked crushed at this response, though for very different reasons. Jason sank back onto his chaise lounge with a sigh, clearly devastated he couldn't escape that easily. Lana still had several shopping bags she'd yet to unbox in front of him.

Iris yelled, "Okay, Gwandmewair! I'll wait for you!"

Michael returned to pulling the twins around the pool on the unicorn floatie while making neighing noises, while I offered to watch Iris do her somersaults. This offer, however, was snubbed. Only Princess Olivia was superior in pool-somersault-watching to Grandmère.

It was only a minute or two later that we all heard the bloodcurdling scream that erupted from the pool house.

Michael was the first one to Grandmère's side, likely because he was the tallest, with the longest legs. He was able to leap over all the chaise lounges in his way and bound inside the pool house before I could even get out of the water.

"I didn't want to say anything before, Mia," Lana said, gesturing to one of the footpersons to bring her a towel so she could dry off her legs, since Michael had gotten them a little wet in his amazing leap from the pool, "but you do have a little bit of a mouse problem. I guess it's to be expected in a castle this old, but Fat Louie has really fallen down on the job in his old age. You should think about getting a younger cat, or maybe an exterminator."

"That wasn't the sound of a woman screaming at the sight of a mouse," I muttered as I heaved myself out of the pool, since this was beginning to appear as if it might be a crisis for which my diplomacy skills would be needed.

"Your grandmother has never screamed at the sight of a mouse in her life," Lilly agreed.

It wasn't a mouse.

This was confirmed when, a moment later, Michael reappeared in the pool house door with my grandmother weeping at his side. She clutched a still-trembling Rommel in one hand and a crumpled piece of palace stationery in the other.

"They're . . . they're gone!" she cried, dramatically sagging in Michael's arms.

I had no idea what she was talking about . . . then. I should have, but I didn't. Back then, I was naive. We all were.

"Who's gone?" I asked, pulling on my beach cover-up. "The boys? They probably just went into town for more beer."

Not to be mean, but I'd never in my life seen anyone consume as much beer as Chad and Derek. Obviously I'd gone to Sarah Lawrence, a formerly all-women's college still attended mostly by females, so I know relatively little about the beer consumption of young men.

Of course, we were living in pandemic conditions, and my own alcohol consumption had increased dramatically, so I wasn't judging. Still, I'd suggested to Grandmère that she might want to ask Derek to make his own liquor runs, just to keep the palace staff from gossiping too much about how often they were having to re-stock beer in the fridge for her new husband-to-be.

But Chad and Derek did not appear to have gone on a beer run into town.

"Chad is still in there," Grandmère cried, crumpling down onto the nearest chaise lounge like a woman who'd had her knees knocked out from under her. And when I heard her next words, I realized why. "It's Derek. Derek has gone . . . forever . . . with Niamh!"

"What?" Lana shot up from her own chaise lounge like a rocket, her eyes wide with horror. "My *nanny* is gone?"

"Where?" Purple Iris cried from the unicorn floatie in the pool. Her lower lip had begun to tremble. "Where's Niamh? Did the bad men at the gate get her?"

"No, no. Niamh's fine." Michael leaned down and gently plucked the piece of palace stationery from Grandmère's hand. "She and Derek left a note. May I read it to them, Clarisse?"

"Why not?" Grandmère flung herself back onto the chaise longue, one arm draped across her forehead (though careful, I noticed, not to muss her brows or disturb her sun hat or sunglasses). "Why shouldn't my humiliation become public knowledge?"

"Er, it's only us, Clarisse," Lilly pointed out. "We're family."

"But my shame is bound to become tabloid fodder soon enough." Grandmère groaned. "Go on, read it to them. Read it!"

Michael cleared his throat and read from the note Grandmère had been holding. I'm attaching a copy below. Grandmère gave it to me with the request to please pass it on to the royal attorneys—aka Lilly—to see if they could "file charges against Derek for false promises, fraud, and intolerable cruelty."

Dear Clarisse (and anyone else to whom this may pertain),

(It was at this point that Lana cried out, "'Anyone else to whom this may pertain'? That's how Niamh refers to us, her employers, who fed and housed her *and* paid her a thousand dollars a week for her childcare services for over a year? I've never felt so betrayed in my life!")

We are so sorry to have to tell you this way, but we just couldn't bear to keep it secret any longer:
Niamh and I are in love.
It's not something we planned. It just happened. My love for music combined with Niamh's love for dance produced a connection too strong to ignore, although we tried for many weeks.

("Weeks?" Grandmère cried. "They've only known each other a few days!"

"Absolutely." Lana was just as outraged as my grandmother. "We haven't been here for weeks."

But as a matter of fact, Lana and her family have been here for exactly four weeks, five days, and seven hours, something only a diarist as dedicated as myself would know.)

And so, although we're aware that what we're doing will cause heartache for many, today we are acting on our feelings, and departing from this beautiful palace now, before any more damage can be done by our love.

Niamh and I are leaving on the first available train for Nice, and from there will fly to Ibiza, where I've accepted a job as a DJ in a popular nightclub, and Niamh will teach restorative movement at a spa.

I hereby return the ring with which I promised to wed you, Clarisse. Know that I will always hold a special place for you in my heart. And please do not think too badly of us. We are young, and only doing what we believe is the right thing—which is following our dreams—while we still can. I'm so sorry for anyone we might have injured along the way.

Sincerely,
Derek Zagorski

As often as Grandmère had irritated me over the past few months (not to mention years), I had to admit I felt sorry for her. That was a brutal letter for anyone to receive, let alone an old woman, even one who happens to be the super privileged (and occasionally super mean) Dowager Princess of Genovia.

And sure, Derek had tried to let her down gently (or as gently as a nineteen-year-old aspiring DJ who was in love with a beautiful Irish nanny could).

But that didn't mean she wasn't right to feel utterly wrecked.

And she looked it.

"Five thousand," Grandmère said, shaking her head. "*Five thousand* cocktail napkins with my initials entwined with that ungrateful boy's."

"Look, Grandmère." I sat down on the chaise lounge beside hers. "Those cocktail napkins aren't going to go to waste. I'm sure Genovia Cares! will be able to use them."

She turned her oversized purple sunglasses toward me. The lenses were so dark, I couldn't see her eyes through them, but I had a feeling if I had, they'd be filled with tears, or at least bitterness. "What will that harridan the baroness say when she hears about this?" she whispered. "Or the contessa?"

Of course. She was worried about what her inFLUENZer friends were going to say. This is what happens when you have friends who only care about partying and the numbers of likes they get on social media (and their ranking on RateTheRoyals).

"What have you always said to me whenever I've had a similar crisis?" I asked. "No one has ever died of embarrassment before. Not once, in the entire history of time."

Grandmère lifted an edge of her long white scarf and dabbed at the corners of her eyes with it. Of course it came away smeared with black mascara.

"That's boredom, Amelia," she corrected me. "No one has ever died of *boredom*, not embarrassment. That's what I told you whenever you began to fidget during your princess lessons. People have certainly died of embarrassment. I believe that's what killed Wallis Simpson in the end, when the truth about her political leanings during the war came out. She didn't die of dementia, as we were all told."

Lilly cleared her throat and said, "Perhaps there's a way we can spin this whole thing so it works to our advantage."

"How?" Grandmère demanded. "How can we possibly spin *this*? I'm a *princess* who's been left at the altar by a man six decades younger than herself."

I thought the "six decades younger" part was being a bit generous, but I said only, "Well, I'm sure we'll think of something."

"Maybe," Boris chimed in, excitedly holding up the ring he'd bought, "Tina will say yes, and then she and I can get married here in Genovia, and we can use all of the champagne you ordered for your wedding, Princess, for ours!"

When we turned to stare at him, the wide smile Boris was wearing began to fade, and he slowly lowered the ring. "Or," he muttered, "maybe not."

I shook my head at him. Would Boris never learn?

"Well." Lana turned toward her husband. "We'd better go start packing."

Jason looked startled. "What? Why?"

"We can't stay here without a nanny, Jason." Lana whipped off her sunglasses and glared at him. "Who's going to look after the children? *You?*"

"Well, no. I thought maybe—"

"*Me?*" Lana's eyes narrowed dangerously.

"Oh." Jason began to back away from his wife. "Yeah. N-no. Sorry, my bad. We n-need to go home and, uh, start interviewing new nannies."

Lana slid her sunglasses back on. "Exactly."

Michael and I exchanged hopeful glances. Was it possible we were finally going to have the palace to ourselves again? Well, to ourselves and Chad and the rest of my extended family, plus Lilly?

It seemed almost too good to be true.

But the truth is . . . things *do* get better. They can be awful for only so long. The sun does eventually come up, even after the longest of nights. And rain does finally stop pouring, even after the fiercest storm.

And according to John M. Barry, whose book I'm *finally* done reading, even if things after the great influenza of 1918 never did go back to what people back then thought of as "normal," they didn't get *worse* . . .

At least until a few years later, when World War II started.

Quarantine Day 255
(for real, I counted)
Poolside Terrace

So many things have happened since I last wrote (which seems like a lifetime ago, but was really just a few days ago). I finally relented to having Paolo touch up my hair, so I'm sitting here with foil all over my head writing this, waiting for the color to take.

- Lana and Jason and their kids are gone.
  - » This is sad for my own kids because they really loved having Purple Iris and Sir Jason Junior stay with us, but good for me, because if I had to hear from Lana one more time about how I ought to "glow up" and start using Botox now to prevent fine lines and wrinkles from developing, I thought I would lose it.

- Boris is gone, too.
  - » He has sworn us all to secrecy about the ring and the house in the Hamptons that

he bought for Tina. It's taking everything in my power not to blurt out to her in our daily FaceTimes about how he plans to re-propose, especially since she still looks so sad.

» But an important part of diplomacy is knowing when *not* to get involved. In the Star Trek universe, this is known as the Prime Directive: never interfere with the development of an alien civilization (and Boris certainly qualifies as an alien). So I'm staying out of it, though every fiber of my being cries out not to. He says he's going to re-propose "when the time is right."

- Chad surprised us all by asking if he could stay here and work as a tutor for Rocky instead of going back to America (or following his traitorous friend Derek to Ibiza).

» Since Chad's major at the University of Florida turns out to be something called "education sciences," and Rocky is doing so terribly with virtual learning, Mom and Dad said yes. It helps of course that Chad is also proficient at Rocky's two main passions in life (soccer and *Call of Duty*), while being decidedly anti-violence, and that Rocky actually listens to him. It also helps that Chad's mother,

Linda, has kept in close touch with us ever since I sent her the fruit basket. She knows Derek's mother, and she confided to me that Derek and Niamh had a massive fight over the musical merits of Enya just a day after arriving in Ibiza, and already split up (information I have not shared with Grandmère). I had no idea that Enya was Irish, and that to disparage her is to disparage the entire population of Ireland (good to know).

- Michael's company publicly announced they'll be offering their intranasal vaccines to health-care and frontline workers and Genovian residents sixty-five and up starting *tomorrow*!!!!
  » The response has been incredibly positive (especially by those sixty-five and up and those who are frightened of needles).

- The first person to receive Michael's company's vaccine will be . . . *the Dowager Princess of Genovia*!!!!!

I had a feeling things were going to start looking up, and they have.

Of course, when Lilly said there was a way to spin the whole Derek dumping Grandmère thing, I didn't think it would be "instead of showing a royal wedding on international television, show the Dowager Princess receiving an intranasal vaccine."

But it certainly seems to be working because now, when any of Grandmère's friends call to ask her how the wedding planning is going, I overhear Grandmère telling them airily, "Oh, the wedding, yes. Well, I'm afraid I've had to put that off for a while. Why? Haven't you heard? I'm to be the first person in Genovia to receive the prince consort's new intranasal vaccine. I know, *cherie*, it's been ages for me, too: I don't think I've put anything up my nose since my Studio Fifty-Four days with that darling Andy Warhol. But I suppose one must make sacrifices for the good of the people, mustn't one? You'll be coming to the after-party, won't you? We're having it at the palace, very exclusive. But it will be outdoors, and you must agree to get the vaccine to attend."

Boom.

No one in Grandmère's circle is mentioning Derek anymore. Instead all they want to talk about is what they're going to wear on the big day (the new designer clothes they've had in the closet since the pandemic began, and been unable to show off until now); how much press is going to be there (*so* much, from all over, because even though we're one of the smallest countries in Europe, we're the first and *only* one to be giving out a nasal vaccine); and what we'll be serving (all the champagne Grandmère ordered for the wedding, along with custom plated hors d'oeuvres that will be served by masked and gloved footpersons).

Of course we're keeping the guest list limited, since Michael says the vaccines don't start working right away. It takes two weeks to build up full immunity.

So we're keeping the attendance to only five of Grandmère's closest InFLUENZer friends . . . the five whose great-grandchildren have the most followers on their social media feeds, so they can help spread the word about how great the vaccine is. Every little bit helps!

I just hope everything goes all right. I'm trying to feel positive about this—and about the fact that I'm getting the vaccine tomorrow, too. As leaders of the country, the prime minister and I qualify as frontline workers. This is the only reason I relented to having my hair done, since I'll be filmed receiving my dose. I'm perfectly fine with my gray, but as Paolo pointed out, "Of course the gray is beautiful, I love the gray, I know many women who look *bellissima* with the gray. But when you *slam* into the gray like you are doing, *principessa*, it look like the train wreck, you know what I am saying? It look better if you *ease* into the gray like a gentle bicycle ride down the Cinque Terre. Trust Paolo. I will take you into the gray so slowly, you will go from a *principessa* to a queen and no one will tell how it happen."

So I'm just trying to relax and not imagine how it's going to feel tomorrow when, right after Grand-mère, I have to go in front of all those cameras and have Michael's vaccine sprayed up my nose.

Michael says the mist is very gentle and I won't feel a thing. Of course he already gave himself the vaccine weeks ago without telling me, before testing it on anyone else, because he wanted to make sure it was safe.

But he's wrong that I won't feel anything because when my pediatrician back in New York prescribed me a nasal spray antihistamine for my springtime allergies, I only used it once before realizing I hate the sensation of anything going up my nose (which was a big disappointment to Lana when I went to visit her at her sorority back when we were both in college).

But for the good of my country, I will inhale Michael's vaccine, and try not to gag on camera.

The only other fly in the ointment (I hate that expression, why am I even using it? What kind of ointment is it, and why is there a fly in it? And is it because I spend so much time around Gen Xers and Boomers that I regularly use expressions like this?) is Prince René.

As soon as Prince René and his fellow protesters down by the palace gates heard about Michael's vaccine (because it's literally been all over the news and social media), they added these signs to their anti-mask signs:

MY NOSE, MY CHOICE!
NO VACCINE NEEDED:
I HAVE AN IMMUNE SYSTEM!
RESIST THE MONARCHY!
WAKE UP, GENOVIA: END THE TYRANNY!
SAY NOSE TO PRINCE MICHAEL!
VACCINATE THE TOURISTS, NOT LOCALS!
FREEDOM OVER FEAR!
PRINCESS MIA WANTS YOUR NOSTRILS!

While I'm glad we've given them something fresh to bond over, I do wish they'd read the actual science behind Michael's vaccine before simply dismissing it. The only side effect is a runny nose and possible sore throat, but the benefits are:

- 99.9 percent protection against death or severe illness from COVID-19

- A higher level of antibodies and stronger mucosal immunity than those, like Chad, who've already had the virus

- A pain-free delivery system (except of course for the discomfort experienced by those, like me, who dislike having things shot up their nose, however gently)

- Protection of the people around you who might be at risk of severe illness, like the elderly, babies, or the immunocompromised

- Stopping the pandemic

Why wouldn't anyone want to help keep babies and sick people safe, and/or help stop this pandemic? It honestly boggles my mind that someone related to me could be so lacking in empathy that they'd—

Oh, Grandmère is demanding that Paolo rinse my hair first since she's on a "very important call" with the Contessa Trevanni about the "vaccine party" tomorrow. More later.

*M*ichael and I were just finishing up the last episode of Season 4 of *The Crown* (oh my God, I will never get over what they did to Diana. Honestly, I shouldn't even watch this show, it is giving me PTSD) when my phone rang.

No one ever calls me after midnight unless it's an emergency, so I was sure it was the prime minister to say something had gone wrong with the vaccine launch—maybe she'd come down with COVID, or some Liechtensteiners had broken into Michael's lab and stolen all the vials of the drug for themselves.

But then I saw that it was Tina.

"Hello?" I was worried something was the matter. Maybe *Tina* had come down with COVID. It was a distinct possibility, given how many hours she spent at the hospital with patients who had the virus.

But the face I saw fill my cell phone screen was glowing with health and happiness.

"Mia?" Tina cried. Literally cried, because Tina was crying, but since she was smiling at the same time, I could tell she was crying with happiness. Also, I caught a glimpse of Boris's dopey face in the background, so I realized exactly why she was calling. "I wanted you to be the first to know!"

I glanced at Michael beside me in bed, and he rolled his eyes and put the chocolate mousse we'd been eating back into the bedside fridge.

"No," I said to Tina, feigning disbelief. "Are you and Boris—?"

"Back together?" Tina shrieked and held her left ring finger up to her phone. On it gleamed the enormous diamond ring Boris had bought her at Jewels of Genovia. "Yes! Yes, we're engaged again. Boris sold the house in Malibu! We're going to live in Manhattan so I can be near the hospital!"

"No way!" I signaled for Michael to bring the mousse back out, but he shook his head. *We're not wasting it*, he mouthed. *It's for watching TV only.*

I couldn't believe he was being such a Mousse Dictator.

"I'm so happy for you, Tina," I said. "I always knew you two would get back together."

"She did!" I heard Boris yell in the background. "Mia, you and Michael have always been our biggest supporters! Thank you!"

"It's nothing," Michael yelled back. "Now go call someone else so we can go to bed. It's two in the morning here."

"Oh, is it?" Tina looked shocked. "Oh my gosh, I forgot about the time difference!"

"It's okay," I said, giving Michael a dirty look. "I want to hear all about the proposal."

"Another time," Tina said, "when it's not so late there. But I do want to tell you—we want to get married in Genovia!"

"Yes," Boris yelled. "Because if it weren't for the two of you, we wouldn't be together now!"

"Oh," I said. "I'm sure that isn't true."

"It's totally true! Mike, tell her." Boris sounded like he'd had a little too much champagne— probably because he had. "Tell her it's true!"

Michael looked at me gravely. "Mia. Boris says it's true."

Out of view of the camera, I slapped his shoulder. Into the phone, I said, "You know you're welcome anytime."

"We don't mean to invite ourselves," Tina said. "But I was thinking something small—maybe just a few friends, in a few months, when everyone's had a chance to get vaccinated and things have opened up again? And in lieu of gifts, we were thinking we could ask everyone to donate to that charity you support, Mia—VOW for Girls, the one you're always going on about that works with families and communities to end the practice of child marriage, and ensure that young girls can stay in school and get job training instead."

I blinked. "Wait. What?"

"You know. Didn't you say twelve million girls a year are forced into underaged marriage around the world? And it's probably even more now with this pandemic and the food shortages and everything?"

"Um," I said. "Yes."

"Well, since we don't need or want gifts, it would mean so much to us to be able to use our celebration as an opportunity to help out some of those girls."

"Oh my God." I was so touched, I didn't quite know what to say. "Tina. That's so generous. Thanks, that would be amazing—"

But she wasn't finished.

"And could you marry us, Mia?" Tina asked. "I mean, that's something you could do, legally, couldn't you? You're the princess, you can do whatever you want, right? It would mean so much to us."

I glanced at Michael uncertainly. We'd spent so many months saying no to things. Now, all of a sudden, thanks to scientists like him and others, our world was opening up again. Were we simply supposed to start saying yes to things again?

It would be so nice to. Especially things as sweet and as unexpected as this.

Michael smiled at me. Encouraged, I turned back toward the screen and said, "Sure. I'll be happy to marry you, Tina. That sounds amazing."

Tina squealed and clapped her hands, while Boris wrapped his arms around her. "Fantastic!

I've got to lock this lady down. I'm not letting her get away this time!"

"Oh, thank you, Mia!" Tina was crying again. "Thank you, Michael! This is the happiest day of my life!"

She'd said that the last time Boris had proposed and she'd said yes, but I decided to let that pass.

"You're welcome," I said. "Good night. Thank you. And congratulations!"

"Good night!"

I ended the call, then sighed. "Did I just make a huge mistake?"

"No. Why?" Michael looked confused.

"We just agreed to let *Boris Pelkowski* have his wedding here!"

"So?"

"So, we just got out of having to throw a massive wedding for my grandmother, and now we've agreed to host one for *Boris P*, the international pop sensation."

"They said they wanted it small."

"Sure, that's what they say *now*. But—"

Michael reached out, snaked an arm around my waist and pulled me close. "Would you, for once in your life, stop worrying about things that haven't even happened yet?"

"Okay, but throwing a wedding for Boris and Tina wasn't exactly how I was planning on spending the next few months."

"Oh, really? How were you planning on spending them?"

"Here at home with you." I laid my head upon his bare chest.

Michael laughed. "I think you're going to get to do that anyway."

"Yes, but *alone* with you. We never get to be *alone*."

"Well," he said, lifting the sheet over his head. "We're alone right now . . ."

I'm so lucky to be married to such an intelligent, sensitive, and really quite limber man.

Quarantine Day 256, 2 p.m.
Poolside Terrace

*W*ell, it happened:

I'm finally vaccinated against COVID-19. With the "Genovian Squirt," as they're calling it in the media, you only need one dose.

Of course it takes the body a couple of weeks to build up full immunity once receiving any vaccination, so it wasn't like I immediately ran around in rapturous joy and kissed all of the photojournalists who were filming us as we got our doses. Most reporters are perfectly nice people who are only doing their jobs—except the ones who write for RateTheRoyals—but I still haven't forgiven them for that time they used that telephoto lens on me when Michael and I were honeymooning on the royal yacht. How dare they accuse me of having a "royal belly bulge"? I was pregnant. With twins! And even if I wasn't, it's no one's business but mine how my belly looks.

Instead I put my mask back on and concentrated on staring up at the sun, because looking up into a bright light is the best way, Grandmère told me long ago, to keep from crying.

And I really wanted to cry, both because I was so deeply moved by what was happening—Drs. Khan and Muhammad looking so brisk and professional in their white coats, walking around and administering the nasal vaccine to the Genovian health-care and frontline workers who'd been chosen for the televised event—and because my eyes were watering like crazy in a reaction to getting something sprayed up my nose. Why can't I be a normal person who reacts to things in a normal way?

But at least I didn't rear back and fall down gagging like I do every time I get a COVID test.

And fortunately I remembered to wear water-proof eyeliner and mascara.

So I don't think anyone noticed that I was standing there with great big glistening Bambi eyes. Well, anyone but Michael, who reached out and took my hand and whispered, "Are you all right?" through his mask.

"Fine," I whispered back, and squeezed his fingers, and pretended like I was simply deeply, deeply grateful for all the work he and his team have done—which I am, I truly am. Leaders from as far away as Japan are already writing to ask if we have vaccine to spare (we do not, but Michael and his team are working 24/7 developing more).

And it feels so nice to have people over at the palace again (even if it is being held strictly out-doors after making sure all who were invited passed a PCR test administered at the door and had also not been around an infected person for the past ten days, and of course the children aren't allowed and are being kept upstairs, entertained by Chad and Olivia and Khalil with the Disney Channel).

But it would have been nice if Michael could have made his spray mint or maybe even grape flavored, because I can feel it dripping down the back of my throat and it really does taste quite medicinal, and not in a delicious cherry throat lozenge way.

But I know I shouldn't complain, because I have so, so much be thankful for. We're all going to LIVE now—and live without this horrible fear hanging over our heads like we have for the past year and even longer, really. We're going to live!

Well, everyone who agrees to get the Genovian Squirt, anyway.

Sadly, this doesn't include certain members of my own family.

"I don't know what's wrong with the boy," I overheard the Contessa Trevanni, one of Grandmère's InFLUENZer friends, telling anyone who'd listen here at the after-vaccine party back at the palace. "It's like he's got a death wish."

"Well, maybe he does, Elena." Baroness Bianca Ferrari was shoveling shrimp cocktail into her mouth. "After all, what does he have to live for, now that Bella is gone?"

"Wait. WHAT?" I could hardly believe my ears. I know eavesdropping is wrong, but this was huge: *"Bella has left Prince René?"*

Grandmère flicked me the same annoyed look she always does when I interrupt her conversations (but her conversations are generally so over-the-top, it's difficult not to be drawn into them).

"Yes, Amelia," Grandmère said in a bored voice after taking a sip from her Sidecar. "Not that it's any of your business, but Bella has filed for divorce from Prince René."

Honestly, this is even bigger than Boris P and Tina Hakim Baba breaking up. My cousin Prince René and his wife, Bella, have a son, Morgan. It's sad when anyone gets divorced, but when a couple *with a kid* splits, it's so much worse . . . unless of course the couple doesn't get along at all, like my mom and dad, who didn't get together until after their child (me) was an adult, much less bother telling her that she was a princess until she was a teen. Not that I have any trauma at all about that.

"Yes, we're all just devastated, Your Highness." Contessa Trevanni—who's had so many face-lifts and so much lip filler that she's begun to resemble a Real Housewife of the Riviera—didn't look very devastated as she shoveled mini crab cakes into her mouth. "But then again, not every couple can be like you and Prince Michael. For some couples, this pandemic has revealed the cracks in their relationship, and they've proven too fragile to withstand the stress of the crisis."

"So true." Baroness Ferrari waved around her

sixth or seventh glass of champagne. "It seems as if young people have been especially unable to maintain their relationships during this difficult time. Wouldn't you agree, Clarisse?"

The Baroness wore an expression of perfect innocence, but I saw Grandmère's eyes flare wide at the catty reminder of her breakup with Derek, and couldn't help feel a little bit sorry for her.

Before I could open my mouth to say a word, however, Lilly was there putting a pretty big dent in her own plate of crab cakes—and the baroness.

"I can't say that I agree." Lilly spoke with her mouth full, as was her custom. "Statistically, people of my generation are actually less likely to get divorced, since they're waiting to marry until they're quite sure of their partner, and therefore also older and finished with their degrees, and more on track with their finances and careers."

The baroness stared at Lilly like she was a creature that had just crawled out of her bathtub drain. "Degrees? Careers? Well, I never—"

"I know, you have neither. But look at Princess Mia and Prince Michael," Lilly went on. She nodded toward her brother, who was standing across the pool beside the prime minister and her husband. Neither Madame Dupris nor I had allowed our children to attend this little soiree, out of concern they might become infected by one of the InFLUENZers (Michael and his team feel confident that his intranasal vaccine will be safe for children—at a smaller dose than adults receive—but they aren't finished testing it yet. I told him to go ahead and test it on the twins since I'm sure nothing will kill them as just the other day I caught them eating the olives out of Dad's martini glass, and they didn't appear any the worse for wear, but he said he would wait until he had more data).

"This crisis has only served to bring the two of them closer," Lilly went on, "because they've been working so hard to help others. I'm guessing if your niece left Prince René, Contessa, it's probably because René is . . . well, he's what he's always been, the same as Derek: a huge screw-up." Lilly lifted her glass of rosé in a toast. "We're better off without those losers. Am I right, ladies? Or am I right?"

Grandmère practically smashed her glass into Lilly's. "You are absolutely *correct*." She rolled all the *rs* in *correct*.

The baroness blinked a few times, looking startled. "Well, I . . . hadn't thought of it that way, I suppose."

"I'm quite sure Prince Morgan doesn't feel that way," the contessa said, looking offended. "One of those 'losers,' as you call him, is the boy's father."

"Yeah," Lilly said. "And René doesn't even care enough about his own child to wear a mask in public or get vaccinated."

"It's an absolutely rotten disgrace!" Grandmère

declared, again rolling her *r*s. She was clearly enjoying herself very much, and not just because she'd been the center of attention all day, what with being the first person in Genovia to get the vaccine, and the fact that everyone was bad-mouthing her most recent ex.

No, other amazing stuff was happening: the successful (so far) launch of Michael's vaccine had sent the Genovian stock market soaring, and tourism, already at record-breaking heights, was skyrocketing as well. We were hearing from the Genovian Hotel and Restaurant Association that reservations were now at all-time highs. The Paninis could hardly make enough paninis to satisfy the hordes of customers at their bakery.

"If Your Graces will excuse us for a moment," I said, taking Lilly by the arm and steering her away from Grandmère and the InFLUENZers, "Lilly and I need to go check on the cake."

Grandmère raised her eyebrows. "There's cake?"

"Of course there's cake! Vaccination cake." I didn't want to tell her that it was in place of the wedding cake that Chef Bernard had been hoarding ingredients for in case she went ahead with the wedding and there were supply issues. "Chef made it special. It will be out in a few minutes. Let me just go and check on it."

"Why do I have to go with you to check on the vaccination cake?" Lilly asked as I dragged her toward the Grand Staircase. "What even is a vaccination cake, anyway?"

"We're not checking on the cake." I was undoing my bra as we walked. It had been so long since I'd worn one, undoing it felt like being liberated from a boa constrictor. "We're going to go talk to my cousin René."

"We're going to go *what*? And excuse me, *but what are you doing*?"

Lilly asked this as we entered my bedroom and I immediately began wiggling out of my Spanx.

"Trust me," I said. "I have a plan."

"What kind of plan? One that involves you walking around without any underwear on?"

"No." I grabbed a pair of sweatpants from my "casual clothes" drawer. "Well, yes, sort of. Remember the other day when we went to Michael's office to see if he was cheating on me with Judith Gershner and no one recognized me?"

"No. You made me go jewelry shopping with Boris and Lana. I had to spend two hours listening to the two of them gush over cruelty-free gemstones."

"Right. Sorry about that. Well, anyway, I was dressed in my normal clothes, and no one recognized me." I tugged my sweatpants on under the silk dress I was wearing. "What if I went out now, dressed the same way, and had a talk with René? A heart-to-heart about the choices he's making?"

"Uh . . . he'd wonder why some weird lady in sweatpants and a Prada dress is talking to him?"

"Obviously I'm ditching the dress." I did just

that, shedding the dress and slipping on my faithful Spice Girls T-shirt and knee-length cardigan.

"Well, okay. Now he's just going to wonder if the 1990s are calling."

I gave her a dirty look as I secured a *Genovia Strong!* baseball hat over my newly blown-out hair. "Thanks. The point is that we're family, and family tries to help one another in times of duress."

"Even if one member of that family is carrying a rifle and has vowed to arrest the other?"

"I've already thought about that," I said. "And that's why you're coming with me as my legal representative, and Lars and Serena are coming as armed protection."

"A wise decision," Lilly said. "But I wouldn't get my hopes up that you're going to change René's mind."

I glared at her. "Whose side are you on, anyway? And are you going out there dressed like that? Everyone is going to recognize you right away. The only other person in Genovia who dresses in business suits is my dad."

She rolled her eyes. "Fine. I'll change. But are you listening to me? Your cousin René is an actual prince—about as entitled and privileged as you can get. There's no way you're going to get him to change his mind on this subject. He believes he's right as strongly as you do. There's nothing you royals value more than your freedom."

"Like . . . our freedom to live without fear of our children coming down with a deadly disease?"

"Actually, yes. On that, you and René might agree."

I handed her a *Genovia Strong!* baseball cap. "Great. Get changed. We're heading out."

Quarantine Day 256, 6 p.m.
Crazy Ivan's

I honestly didn't think I'd be spending any part of the day I received my COVID vaccine sitting on the rooftop terrace of Genovia's most popular nightclub, owned by my cousin, Count Ivan Renaldo.

But here I am.

I guess when you're in the middle of a global pandemic, things can be unpredictable.

And fortunately it's unlikely anyone will recognize me in my baseball cap and mask, especially since I'm sitting here with my cousin Ivan, who everyone in Genovia knows I can't stand.

But right now I have to admit Ivan might be one of my favorite people (Michael and my children aside, of course).

And that's because, for perhaps the first time in his life, Ivan is actually doing me a favor.

Lilly is the one who made me think of asking him for it. When she was squawking back at the palace about how there was no way I was ever going to change my cousin René's mind on the masking/vaxxing issue, I thought to myself, *Actually, there is.*

Because my cousin Ivan had changed *his* mind on those very same topics—but only after coming down with a case of COVID so awful, he had to be hospitalized with it.

Obviously Ivan is out of the hospital now, but he's a changed man. So changed that Ivan now not only requires all of his employees to wear masks, he asks customers to wear them, too (except while eating and drinking). He even requires his topless dancers to wear masks (for their own protection, he says, and that of their customers).

That's why, when I quietly approached René by the palace gate and said, "René, it's me. Don't make a big deal out of this. Let's go somewhere and talk," and he finally recognized me and blurted, wide-eyed, "What? Oh. Okay. Where?" I said, "Crazy Ivan's."

I don't know what he was expecting. I mean, he and his buddies had been standing outside the palace for weeks—months, even—and I'd been steadily ignoring them. Then on the day we release our vaccine, I just walk up to him (in disguise), flanked by armed Genovian Guards (also in disguise, though I have to say that as much as Lars tried to make himself look like a German tourist, the cargo shorts and leather sandals weren't fooling anyone, since it was quite obvious—to me, anyway—that he had both a taser and a pistol in the fanny pack he was wearing around his waist, as did Serena).

But maybe the baroness was right, and René was in tons of emotional pain over the breakup of his marriage, since all he said to me was "All right."

Then he handed his sign—*My Nose, My Choice*—and hunting rifle to a fellow protester and fell in step behind us.

"Don't get too close to me," René said as we began walking down Rue de Princesse (or Princess Street) toward Crazy Ivan's. "Your disguise isn't that good. I don't want any of my friends to realize I'm consorting with the enemy."

"Sure." Like I was so eager for any of *my* friends—or the general public—to think I liked being seen with someone like him.

"So we hear things aren't going so well with your marriage," Lilly blurted out.

I gave her a warning look. Bluntness works well in the legal profession but in my line of work, it's the opposite.

"What are you talking about?" René was looking everywhere except our faces. "Things are fine between Bella and me, couldn't be better."

"Really, Your Highness?" Lilly shook her head. "That's why you've been standing outside the Royal Palace for so many days on end holding a dopey sign, instead of enjoying your happy marriage to your gorgeous wife?"

"Some of us," René said with a condescending sniff, "are critical thinkers who are willing to sacrifice our own comfort and personal happiness for a greater cause."

"Why don't you cut the crap? We got it straight from the horse's mouth—your grandmother-in-law—how Bella got sick and tired of hearing your anti-science rhetoric, so she left you and took Morgan with her. Or did she kick you out? If I were her, I'd have changed the locks and thrown all your stuff out onto the street, then lit it on fire for good measure."

René froze so suddenly, I almost slammed into him. His eyes went as wide as when he'd first seen me, and his cheeks went as red as his plaid shirt.

"That—that's not what happened!" he sputtered in so horrified a manner, I was certain that was exactly what had happened.

"Of course it's not, René." I laid a comforting hand on his arm while giving Lilly the evil eye. "We're actually here to listen, not judge. I'm sure the things the contessa said aren't true—"

"They aren't!" he cried. "Bella and I are still blissfully in love. I see my boy every weekend. Well, every other weekend. I'm actually very busy. A lot of people are depending on me to get our message out—"

"Of course they are." We'd reached the doors to Crazy Ivan's by that point, which is where I pulled out my cell phone and began texting, ignoring a text from Michael inquiring, Where are you? "Could you hold on a minute?" I asked René. "There's someone else from our family who wants to say hello."

René glanced at the sign above us that screamed:

**WELCOME TO CRAZY IVAN'S
-HOME OF THE WORLD-FAMOUS SUNDOWNER-
WE'VE GOT SOMETHING FOR EVERYONE!
OFFERING A FUSION OF HIGH-CLASS
ENTERTAINMENT WITH BEACHSIDE FUN,
IVAN'S IS *THE* PLACE IN GENOVIA TO SEE
AND BE SEEN. WITH A DJ SPINNING ALL
OF EUROPE'S LATEST HITS, FIVE DISCO
FLOORS, STATE-OF-THE-ART LIGHTS
AND LASER SHOW, AND A ROOFTOP
LOUNGE OVERLOOKING GENOVIA'S DEEP
BLUE BAY AND WHITE-SAND BEACH,
YOU'LL ALWAYS BE GLAD
YOU GOT CRAZY AT
CRAZY IVAN'S!**

"Wait. Is it Count Ivan?" René asked. "You didn't drag me all the way here to speak to Count Ivan, did you?"

"What?" I laughed nervously as Michael texted again: I'm serious. WHERE ARE YOU? "No way!"

A second later, Ivan came down the carpeted steps from the lobby of his club to greet us. Sixty pounds lighter than before the pandemic (and not in a good way), he nevertheless cut a striking figure with his white tuxedo and silver cane.

"Cousin!" Ivan cried. "And *cousine*! How are

you? Welcome, welcome! It's so good to see you both!" Ivan flung his free arm around a startled-looking René's neck and hugged him. "What?" he asked, when René tried to pull away. "You don't recognize me, or you think I'm still contagious? I'm not, I'm not. And I have this mask on, I always wear it, because I care about my loved ones. I almost died, you know. Princess!" Ivan kissed the air around my head through his mask. "Such a pleasure. I never get to see you anymore! But then, I know, motherhood. And the throne! They keep a woman busy. Come in, come in, I had them reserve my best table—"

And that's where we've been sitting ever since, overlooking the beach and the Bay of Genovia, while waitresses come by bringing us Sundowners—Crazy Ivan's most controversial cocktail yet: a delicious mix of champagne, orange liqueur, grapefruit juice, and absinthe, served with a silver straw for easy sipping while masked—and white yachts sail past on the turquoise water, and Ivan tells René about his bout with COVID and his hospital stay, exactly as I wanted him to.

"I kept telling everyone who would listen, 'It's nothing but the flu,'" Ivan said in a voice that was a pale echo of his former baritone. "Remember, Princess, I was always saying that? 'All this fuss about a flu!'"

"I do remember," I said.

No worries, I texted Michael. Had to run to the pharmacy

with Lilly. She's having some lady trouble. Serena and Lars are with us. All good.

Michael texted back:

> You've never been a very good liar.

Uh-oh.

"But this," Ivan went on. "This was no flu! They had to put a tube down my throat to help me breathe!"

René didn't look convinced. "But, no offense, Ivan, it's not as if you were so healthy to begin with. It's pretty well-known that the virus doesn't affect young people like me, who are in good condition."

"Where on earth did you get that idea, boy?" Ivan laughed at René as if he'd said something as ridiculous as *The moon is made of Gruyère cheese.* "The fellow in the bed next to me in the hospital—he was about your age, René, and he had to have a lung transplant. Saddest thing I've ever seen, his poor wife and daughter not being able to come into the hospital to visit him—"

René blinked a few times. "Yes, but he probably lived an at-risk lifestyle. Didn't eat healthfully, or take vitamins, like I do."

I gasped. "René!" Maybe this had all been a mistake. Maybe Bella had been right to change the locks and throw all his stuff out onto the street, because he was beyond saving.

"You know that I have a green smoothie every morning, first thing," René insisted. "When Bella and I were still together, we observed a strict vegan diet—"

Ivan's fist came sailing down onto the tabletop, causing such a loud thump that Lars and Serena both went reaching for their belt bags.

"What does that matter?" Ivan roared. "People are dying! What's wrong with you, boy? Can you not feel anything for anyone but yourself?"

René didn't even have the decency to look ashamed of himself. Instead, he appeared sullen. "No. I mean, yes, I can feel things for people besides myself. I'm just saying, scientifically, the chances of my getting seriously ill from COVID are very—"

"And I'm just saying, *scientifically*, what about your little boy? Do you think your wife is feeding *him* green smoothies every morning? Personally, I've never met a little kid who likes them." Ivan dug his cell phone from his pocket. "This is how I ended up." He showed us a photo of himself in the ICU. He was hardly recognizable, there were so many tubes going in and out of him. "I wouldn't wish this on anyone else."

"Whoa." Lilly pointed at something in the photo. "Is that a bag of pee hanging by the side of your bed?"

"Yes." Ivan chuckled ruefully. "I was too weak to make it to the toilet, so they had to stick a catheter up my—"

"All right." René leaped from the table. "That's enough. I get what you're trying to do. But that photo has obviously been faked!"

Ivan shook his head as he put his phone away. "I'm sorry, Amelia. I tried."

I sighed. "I know. Thanks."

René looked from me to Ivan and then back again. "What do you mean, you tried? Were you two in on this together? Was this some kind of *conspiracy*?"

"If you mean a conspiracy to get you to show sympathy and caring for your fellow man, then yes, René," I said. I couldn't believe my lovely plan both to reunite my family and put an end to René's absurd protest had failed. "But it obviously didn't work, because you have neither. That was a real photo, but you just accused your own cousin, a man who nearly died, of faking it. Why on earth would he do that? Why would he go to the trouble? Did he fake his weight loss, too? His obviously unhealthy pallor?"

Count Ivan appeared offended. "Hey! I don't look *that* bad." He turned to Serena. "Do I?"

She looked uncertain how to reply. "Er . . ."

"What would Ivan possibly have to gain?" I barreled on. "He's a businessman. He doesn't have time for that kind of nonsense. Why would he have faked any of this?"

For the first time, René looked uncertain. "Well . . . I don't know. But big pharma—"

"Oh, *shut up*, René." Lilly rose from her chair

in distaste. "Come on, Mia, let's go. This is point-
less. I'm pretty sure there's nothing more we can
say to this clown that's going to make any difference. If he wants to die, let him. I just hope he
doesn't take anyone with him on his way out."

A shadow fell across our table, which had
turned as orange in the warm rays of the setting
sun as our cocktails. "For once I agree with my
sister."

I was startled by the deep—and oddly
familiar—masculine voice. It wasn't until I
turned and saw the person to whom it—and the
shadow—belonged that I realized why:

"Michael?"

To say I was shocked to see my husband standing on the rooftop of Crazy Ivan's would be an understatement.

"How did you find us?" I thought I'd been really cagey with my text about the pharmacy.

"Did you forget that the Genovian Guard activated the Find My Friends function on all our phones in case we're ever kidnapped?" Michael pulled out a chair, spun it around, then sat in it backwards, facing René with a steely, Keanu-Reeves-in-*John-Wick* stare.

Although I'm not normally a fan of movies in which dogs die, I have to say I'm a big fan of that one.

René, for his part, had grown quite pale upon seeing Michael—so pale that he seemed to lose the use of his limbs, and so sank bonelessly back down into his own chair, shrinking a little behind Lars as if for protection. Which was ludicrous, because mere seconds before Lars had been the one on the verge of tasering him.

"You Found My Friends me?" I couldn't believe

it. I thought our marriage had been built on a foundation of trust (even though I had recently suspected him of having an affair with his geneticist ex-girlfriend and had been lying my face off to him via text less than an hour earlier).

. "Not me." Michael's gaze never wavered from René. "Your sister, Olivia. She noticed you'd been gone an awfully long time for someone who'd only slipped out to buy tampons. She checked her Find My Friends app, then alerted everyone to the fact that you were here. Olivia wants to know if you've lost your mind, and if so, if she's now in charge of the country, as she's third in line to the throne after the twins, and they're too young to rule."

I frowned. Of course. Typical reasoning for a straight-A student like Olivia.

"I, uh, think I'd better go." René, seeming to have recovered use of his extremities, began to scramble for the exit, but Lars, who was closest to him, reached over with one hand and pushed him wordlessly down into his seat again.

"Oh, don't go," Ivan cried. "Stay and try the calamari!" He didn't seem to be sensing the tension in the air among myself, Michael, and René. He genuinely wanted us to stay and try his fried squid. "I've tweaked the recipe. I want to see if you can tell the difference. Claudia!" Ivan waved to our waitress. "A basket of calamari for my guests!"

Claudia nodded and hurried to the kitchen to deliver her boss's order.

"I'm not sharing calamari with *him*." Michael pointed at Prince René.

Ivan spread his arms open wide. "Oh, come now. Do you know what my near-death experience taught me? That life is too short for family squabbles and disagreements. All this division is bad for the digestion."

"Family squabbles?" Michael spoke very calmly, but I could see the fury smoldering in his eyes. "This man threatened to make a citizen's arrest of my wife for crimes against the state, when everything she does is for the good of her country and its people. He's lucky I haven't thrown him over the side of this roof yet."

René shrank even farther behind Lars, who scooted his chair away from him in response. "L-look, I've been meaning to apologize for all that," René said. "We were never *actually* going to arrest you, Princess. We were really only trying to get our point across."

"Your *point* being that you are immoral, willfully ignorant, gaslighting misogynists?" Lilly asked.

René's discomfort turned to confusion. "No. That we have a right to individual freedom."

"*Freedom* to keep our hospitals overwhelmed with the infected?" Michael asked. "*Freedom* to continue to force children to attend school virtually? *Freedom* to create new variants of the virus because you refuse to mask or be vaccinated, so the pandemic continues forever? Yes, you absolutely do have those rights and that freedom. The question I have is what kind of person would make those choices, especially when the moral alternative is clear?"

René just sat there with his mouth hanging open like Grandmère's dog, Rommel, when he was eyeing a piece of cheese he couldn't reach. My cousin seemed to be searching his brain for some kind of retort to Michael's question, but he simply didn't have the synaptic firepower to keep up with him. Claudia the server had to nudge him gently out of the way as she arrived with the basket of calamari.

"Here you go," she said cheerfully, setting it down on the center of our table. "Bon appétit!"

"Ah!" Ivan was overjoyed. "Now try this and tell me what you think."

Serena dunked a crispy piece of calamari into the red sauce that came with it. "The breading is so light!"

Lars frowned as he chewed. "It does have a remarkably airy texture."

Ivan grinned. "I told you! It's my new recipe. Can you guess? Can you guess what it is?"

"Cornstarch?" I asked, chewing. "You use cornstarch instead of flour?"

Ivan laughed. "Cornstarch, no! It's *panko*. Panko, the Japanese breadcrumbs! They're the lightest, airiest breadcrumbs, and make for the best calamari, in my opinion."

"Oh, fine!" René leaped from his chair. Michael's

psychological torture had worked. "You're right. I've been a fool. A stupid, selfish fool. I never wanted to arrest Mia in the first place. I don't even want to protest anymore! Do you have any idea what it's like to stand all day out there in the hot sun with those idiots? I want to sit up here and drink champagne punch with all of you and have fun! I want my wife back. I want to see my son. I want to get the Genovian Squirt." He plunged his hand into the center of the calamari basket, then stuffed what he'd grabbed into his mouth and cried, "I don't want to be vegan anymore!"

We watched in shocked silence as he chewed and wept . . . all of us except Count Ivan, who said, "Well, if you like the calamari, you have to try the stuffed mushrooms."

"Uh, no," I said, rising from my chair. "I think we ought to go—"

"I insist!" Ivan clapped his hands. "Claudia! Bring us a basket of stuffed mushrooms. And another calamari. This man is hungry, look at him!"

So that's how we ended up sitting there as René polished off another basket of calamari, a basket of mushrooms, a pizza margherita, and several more Sundowners before he worked up the nerve to call Bella and tell her that he was a changed man who wanted to come home.

I have no idea what Bella said, but it must have given René hope, since he dried his eyes and thanked us, saying that he needed to go.

"And I apologize, Your Highness," he said to me, taking my hand and bowing over it, "for anything I might have done over the past few months to cause you or your family discomfort. I believe I was out of my head with worry and alarm—"

"Classic C and C," Lilly muttered beside me.

"—but of course," René continued, not having heard her, "that is no excuse. In the future, I will endeavor to do as you advised, and think of others before myself."

His gaze strayed toward Michael, who was still sitting and glaring at him, his arms crossed over his chest in that way some men do that causes their biceps to bulge alarmingly, even if they don't actually have the hugest biceps because they spend most of their day in a lab working on computers.

"I think that would be wise," I said to René, and he rather hastily left.

"Shall I follow him, Your Highness?" Lars asked. "Make sure he doesn't double back to the front gates and cause more trouble? Or I could arrest him, take him back to the headquarters of the Royal Genovian Guard, and interrogate him to find out what else he and his 'fellow freedom fighters' might have up their sleeves."

But I told Lars that wouldn't be necessary. I couldn't help feeling as I sat there looking out over the water as the setting sun turned the horizon from blue to purple to fiery gold that something extraordinary was happening. Not the same old extraordinary thing that happened every time the sun went down, signaling that the long day was finally over, and it was time to rest. But something different . . . something better.

"I feel like things are going to be all right . . . like there's hope again," I said to Michael later as we strolled hand in hand back to the palace. There was no need to worry about anyone recognizing us, even though there were tons of other people strolling around us, enjoying the mild evening air. With me in my mask and *Genovia Strong!* hat and him in his mask and his beard and sideburns, we were barely recognizable as the Princess and Prince Consort of Genovia.

Besides, Lars, Serena, and Lilly were right behind us, so if some kind of alien invasion or dance flash mob broke out, we were well protected.

"You feel like things are going to be all right because your cousin's agreed to try not to be so self-centered," Michael said, "and gone back to his wife?"

"No. Well, partly that. But also because your vaccine is going to save thousands of lives. Did you know every single appointment to get it between now and next year is completely filled? They're having to turn away non-Genovians! I hear the Monaco side of my family is really mad because they can't get the Genovian Squirt."

Michael winced. "You know the vaccine has

an actual name. It's not really called the Genovian Squirt."

"It isn't?" Somehow I'd missed this.

"No, it isn't." He squeezed my hand. "It's called
Genflomia."

"GenFLOmia?" I didn't want to offend him,
but this was a terrible name. Why are names for
medications always so terrible? It's even worse
in the US where they allow advertisements for
them on television, and the little jingles for them
get stuck in your head, and you find yourself
singing a tune about a diabetes medication while
you're in the shower shaving your legs.

"Yes," Michael said. "Genflomia. *Gen* for Genovia, *Flo* because it's a mist, and *Mia* for you. Because you and the twins were all I was thinking
about while I was working on it, and how empty
my life would be without you."

And right then and there, I decided that I loved
the name Genflomia.

"Oh, *Michael*," I cried, and spun around in the
middle of the pedestrian crossway, threw my
arms around him, pulled down his mask and
then my own, and kissed him.

If Michael was startled—in a good way—that
was nothing compared to how startled the other
people in the crossway were when my *Genovia
Strong!* hat got accidentally knocked off when I
hit it against Michael's forehead, and all of my
newly dyed and blown-out hair came tumbling
down, and they recognized who I was.

"Look!" a kid holding gelato on a cone cried, pointing at us. "It's Prince Michael and Princess Mia!"

"Princess Mia!" Suddenly a lot of cell phone cameras were pointing our way.

But Michael didn't care. He kept right on kissing me.

And I kissed him right back.

About the Author

Meg Cabot's many books for both adults and teens have included numerous #1 *New York Times* bestsellers, selling over twenty-five million copies worldwide. Her Princess Diaries series was made into two hit films by Disney. She lives in Key West, Florida, with her husband.

Meg is donating ten percent of her proceeds of the sale of this book to VOW for Girls.